SWEET HUMPHREY

Recent Titles by Peter Turnbull from Severn House

The Hennessey and Yellich Series

SWEET HUMPHREY

Peter Turnbull

This first world edition published in Great Britain 2006 by
SEVERN HOUSE PUBLISHERS LTD of
9–15 High Street, Sutton, Surrey SM1 1DF.
This first world edition published in the USA 2006 by
SEVERN HOUSE PUBLISHERS INC of
595 Madison Avenue, New York, N.Y. 10022.

British Library Cataloguing in Publication Data

Turnbull, Peter, 1950-
   Sweet Humphrey
  1.   Serial murderers - Mental health - Fiction
  2.   York (England) - Fiction
  3.   Detective and mystery stories
  I.   Title
  823.9'14 [F]

  ISBN-10: 0-7278-6339-8

Typeset by Palimpsest Book Production Ltd.,
Polmont, Stirlingshire, Scotland.
Printed and bound in Great Britain by
MPG Books Ltd., Bodmin, Cornwall.

One

Inside, the building was airy, plenty of natural light, pastel shades, inmates were addressed by their Christian names, food was excellent, there was therapy, recreation, visits by next of kin . . . it was, after all, a hospital. Outside, the building was austere, red brick, regimented lines, approached via a long driveway, with staff residential quarters on either side, neatly tended lawns and privet hedges. It was a hospital where the nurses were members of the Prison Officers' Union. It was Kempton Hospital, East Yorkshire.

The man turned his car into the driveway and drove slowly towards the main entrance. He parked in the designated visitors' car park and walked to the huge doorway, which he had always found imposing, as if to keep people out, he thought, as much as it was to keep patients in. He rang, and the door was opened inwardly almost the instant that he pressed the bell. The uniformed officer smiled and nodded at the man and stood aside to allow him ingress. The man stepped into the reception area and surrendered his briefcase to be searched and, taking his car keys from his pocket, stood still whilst a metal detector was passed over his body. He stepped forward to the nurse who was logging all visitors.

'Dr Simnal,' he said. 'Maurice Simnal, to see Humphrey Sweet.'

'Sweet, Humphrey,' the officer wrote in the log. 'Aye, we'll escort you over there, Dr Simnal.'

Another nurse escorted Simnal through the labyrinthine

corridors of the hospital and exited into an area in the hospital grounds on which had been built a very modern building of graceful lines and costing, as Simnal had learned, some twenty million pounds, or nearly one million pounds for each of the patients it held. The sign above the main door of the new building read, 'Dangerous and Severe Personality Disorder Unit'.

'Hospital within a hospital,' the nurse who had escorted Simnal to the DSPD sighed, 'and here I leave you, sir . . . thankfully. No offence to you, but me, I wouldn't work there for a pension. Not amongst that lot.'

Simnal turned and smiled. 'Don't think I'd want to either, but visiting for an hour a week . . . I can cope with that, though I still take it, or him, home with me. He has that influence.'

'Humphrey? Aye, he's a bad lot. He has to be double watched . . . no nurse is allowed to be alone with him.'

'So I believe.'

'They find they give in to his requests.'

'So I have heard.'

'One nurse found himself smuggling stuff in for him.'

'Really?'

'Yes . . . when Humphrey was first admitted, or shortly after, found himself reporting for duty one day carrying a blade into the unit . . . stopped himself, said, "What am I doing?"'

'Good for him.'

'Aye . . .' The nurse and Simnal stopped at the entrance to the DSPD unit. 'Went to see his boss, the whole thing was reported to the top. The nurse kept his job but was moved off the DSPD. After that, no nurse is allowed to be alone with him . . . he can manipulate one . . . but not two.'

Simnal raised an eyebrow. 'That you know of.'

The nurse's jaw slackened as she held eye contact with Simnal. 'I hope you're wrong there, sir.'

'I hope so too.'

'Well, it seems to be working because Humphrey is not a happy man . . . so I've heard.'

'That's a good sign. I mean, if he was happy and content, it would be because he was controlling someone.'

'Aye . . . since you put it like that, sir, but if he can do that to a nurse, an experienced nurse as well . . . what chance had those little girls got?'

'None,' Simnal replied as the nurse turned and walked away, his soft-soled shoes making no sound as he headed across the concrete path.

Simnal waited. He glanced about him. It was early June, warm, a high blue sky. It was times like this, in the premises of a secure unit, whether a hospital or prison, that he cherished his own liberty. The little things . . . being able to go for a walk, eat what and when he chose, to dress as he pleased within conventional reason and acceptance . . . little things, but hugely important and which could be lost in an instant. The door was opened and Simnal, nodding his thanks to the nurse who opened it, stepped into the DSPD, viewing its very high ceilings, designed thus to allow a sense of space and reduce the sense of oppressiveness. He signed in at the reception desk and was escorted to the office of the duty psychologist, where he tapped on the door and a female voice invited him to enter.

It was one of the meetings of minds. Maurice Simnal and Ruth Day had liked each other the moment they had met. The attraction had been both strong and mutual, each warmed to the other and each looked at the other with dilated pupils. They had never met socially, and the rocks and bands on the fingers of Ruth Day's left hand said they probably, nay certainly, never would; yet both felt a sense of 'if only we had met earlier'.

'Please . . .' Ruth Day indicated the chair in front of her desk. 'How's the Home Office treating you?'

'Like a dog . . .' Simnal sat in the chair. 'How has our friend been behaving?'

'Worryingly normal . . . worryingly quiet and co-operative.' She opened the drawer of her filing cabinet and took out the file marked 'Sweet, Humphrey'. 'Don't like it when they are like that.'

'Understandable . . . manipulating through obedience.'

'Exactly.' She closed the drawer and sat behind her desk. Simnal saw a slender woman in her late thirties, conservatively dressed with a calf-length skirt and polo neck sweater, hair cut short, spectacles dangling from her neck ready to be put on whenever she had to read something. She was the same age as Simnal, almost to the day . . . which, while never mentioned, they both felt was something else that they had in common, something else that caused them both to feel a sense of frustration about what might have been. 'And the worrying thing is that other patients have followed suit . . . there has been no disruption in the unit since your last visit . . . not a word out of place for nearly two weeks. The nurses are being excellent, they know the danger signs . . . being extra diligent . . . watching out for each other . . . but the danger is that they will become complacent, then all sorts of contraband will be smuggled in as it was in Liverpool . . . including children, for the delectation of the paedophiles. But as I say, the staff are well on their toes . . . but it's early days . . . it took months for the patients in Liverpool to make their nurses drop their guard.'

'Chilling.'

'Oh, yes . . .' Ruth sank back in her chair. 'Our patients are nothing if not intelligent, they are fully able to organize themselves . . . if they weren't so dangerous . . .'

'They'd be university teachers or running the country. So, what has he done?'

'Very little of note.' Ruth read the file. 'As you'll see, fully co-operative . . . contributes to the group therapy sessions . . .' She turned the file round and handed it to Simnal.

'Not a management problem either, I'll be bound.' Simnal reached forward and took the file from her.

'Not at all . . . Mr Co-operative.' Ruth Day reclined in her chair and pondered Simnal. Privately she thought how similar to her brother he seemed, the calm, self-assured manner, the neat face, the large, bold, light framed spectacles, the clean blond hair, the lightweight summer suit. He was, she thought, the image of a man who could warmly welcome her at a restaurant. But no superficially friendly door-to-door salesman he . . . she had realized that from the moment they met. 'And, like I said, seems to be taking the other patients with him.'

'He's the top cat?'

'No, but Mr Mulligan, his charge nurse, seems to think he wants to be . . . and of course nobody here . . . that is to say none of the patients, cares about what he did . . . they have done equal if not worse. This isn't a prison.'

'Yes . . . he'd be segregated if he was inside, doubt if that would protect him even then. I mean, three schoolgirls . . . he'd get the treatment if he was inside.'

'As we both know. That's the one thing that the patients I hear are genuinely frightened of . . . being reclassified as sane and transferred to a prison. It's not the harsher and crowded conditions . . . but the violence which will be coming their way.'

'I can imagine.'

'Those over or approaching fifty can hope for the "Grey House" in the south of England, but for those in their twenties and thirties the prospect of going back to the mainstream is a real terror for them.'

'Yes . . .' Simnal glanced over the ward recordings of the last seven days. 'He's had a visitor, I see.'

'Yes.'

Simnal turned to the back of the file and read the copy of the Visiting Order. 'Kathleen Hood of Selby. What do you know of her?'

5

'Not a great deal. The hospital takes an interest in those visiting its high profile, recently admitted, patients like Sweet . . . as do the police . . . we notified them of her visit. What, if anything, they did, I don't know. We'll just have to see if she visits again. Probably a groupie.'

'It's very strange . . . the more extreme a person's behaviour, the more some people find them fascinating.'

'Well documented.' Ruth Day grimaced. 'I was talking on the phone to a psychologist in Rampton, just recently. He told me of the visitors and the letters that the Yorkshire Ripper receives . . . it's like a fan club. Merits a research project in its own right. What will you be doing with him this afternoon?'

'Sweet? Hope to begin to get down to the nitty-gritty. Last week and the week before we were just establishing a rapport . . . you know the model . . . but he makes me feel very uneasy, so good looking, so pleasant and charming . . . mind you, they all are.'

'Indeed. The Hunchback of Notre Dame with a harsh, rasping regional accent couldn't charm anybody into his car, let alone three schoolgirls.'

'Well,' Simnal placed the file back on Ruth Day's desk, 'I'll go and see him.' He stood.

Ruth also stood. 'I'll walk along with you.'

'You don't have to, but thank you.'

Ruth fell into step with Simnal as they walked down the corridor towards the agents' rooms and he noticed how both he and she allowed their bodies to brush against each other as they proceeded. They reached the ward and Ruth rang the bell. A male nurse responded quickly and unlocked the door.

'Dr Simnal to see Humphrey Sweet,' Dr Day said as they stepped into the ward.

'Yes, ma'am.' The nurse smiled approvingly at Simnal. 'I'll go and bring him to you. He's in art therapy at the moment. Quite a painter.'

6

'Really?' Simnal asked. 'I'd like to see some of his work.'

'It's . . .' Ruth Day moved her head from side to side. 'How would you describe it, David?'

'Weird,' the nurse, 'David' by the name tag on his starched white tunic, grinned. 'But then, that's what you get paid the big bucks for . . . to decipher that . . . anyway, I'll go and fetch him.' David walked away down the ward of comfortable-looking pine beds arranged in rows at ninety degrees from the wall, 'Nightingale' style. The floor was of sealed parquet sections, the windows tall, looking out over a green space to a stand of shrubs beyond which was another section of the DSPD unit. Simnal found it pleasantly cool in the ward. It was evident to him that the windows on the DSPD units were permanently shut and so air conditioning was essential. 'Surprised at the floor,' he said, for want of something to say to Ruth Day.

'The parquet?'

'Yes.'

'Well, wouldn't be used in a prison . . . could easily be torn up and used in a riot despite the generous varnish seal, but our patients are not dangerous in that sense, as you know.'

'Yes, I suppose. Prisoners are more honest in their anti-authority stance.'

'Exactly . . . these are patients. They are on the DSPD because their danger is their calm, their charm, their premeditative manipulation. We just don't know what they're thinking. They are not going to be violent towards authority. They'll murder your child and smile as they spill his blood . . . but will come quietly when arrested. The nurses here can turn their backs on the patients, especially the patients in this wing who are controlling and policing themselves. A warder in a prison couldn't do the same. Well, I'll leave you . . . do call in when you have finished this session. I'd like to hear how it went.'

'Yes.' Simnal and Ruth held eye contact and smiled at each other. 'Yes, I'll do that. I'd appreciate a debrief, help me get my thoughts in order. Well, I'll go and wait in there . . .'

Simnal walked into the small room, which stood near the entrance to the ward and contained just two chairs set at angles to each other. It smelled homely, rather than of a hospital. Impressionist prints hung on the wall, the floor was carpeted, plant pots containing cacti stood on the windowsill, a large pane of glass showed a view of the nursing station and the ward beyond. What was said in the agents' room could not be heard, but the room could be supervised in the unlikely event of a patient 'kicking off'.

Simnal sat in the chair facing the door, again not a good idea in a prison because the interviewee is then sitting between the interviewer and the door and thus in a position to frustrate escape or rescue, should the inmate be inclined to violence. But as Dr Day had said, this was the DSPD unit and the patients here are clever enough to know the importance of co-operation. The danger they present had a subtle, sugar-coated manifestation.

The nurse, David, escorted Humphrey Sweet to the agents' room, walking behind him. At the door, unseen by Sweet, he nodded to Simnal and indicated to his left to the nursing station as if to say, 'I'll be right outside'. Simnal invited Sweet to sit down and, as Sweet's head was momentarily bowed when in the act of sitting, he mouthed 'thank you' to the nurse who quietly withdrew, shutting the door behind him.

'So,' Simnal spoke with a practised mixture of authority and warmth. Sweet was not a man who could be given unqualified approval. Such approval would negate all the work done in the group therapy sessions to make Sweet, and patients like him, confront their offending, to think of the damage they have done, and it would also allow a channel of collusion to open between psychologist and patient: potentially very dangerous. Simnal knew that, but he also knew he needed Sweet to talk to him, he needed the man's co-operation, and so he could not allow hostility and outright disapproval to enter his voice. It was a fine line and he had to tread it. He felt he had the balance judged correctly. Sweet was continuing to agree to see him and yet equally, hadn't attempted to 'draw him in' with that look which he and others of his ilk can use to such devastating effects on vulnerable people, particularly children. That look which enabled Sweet to make people do what they knew to be wrong, yet did it nonetheless. No wonder, Simnal thought, no wonder he had been such a successful salesman. 'How's life in here?'

'Routine,' Sweet smiled. 'But I get by.'

'Dr Day said you are co-operating well.'

Sweet curled his lips, not a smirk, but not a smile, somewhere between the two – but Simnal saw the smirk more than he saw the smile. He also noticed the brief breaking of eye contact that accompanied it. He thought then that the hospital had an awful lot of work ahead of it with respect to Humphrey Sweet, if indeed work could be done. It may be that he would be deemed 'beyond therapy' and given no more than basic caring, three meals a day, a bed, washing facilities, a library to visit, and a television to watch, until he drew his last breath. There were however many days, nay years, before that decision would be taken, if ever. On that afternoon it was early days, still within twelve months of his conviction and subsequent transfer to a 'secure psychiatric facility' under the terms of the Mental Health (Dangerous Offenders) Act. Sweet then made eye contact with Simnal and asked 'How's life for you?'

Interesting, Simnal thought. It was interesting how he suddenly felt cared for by Sweet, a totally misplaced feeling, he knew, because Sweet had murdered three times, because Sweet cared for nobody but himself . . . but nonetheless Simnal felt that this creature cared for him, and following that sudden feeling of being cared for, he felt a certain dependency on him. Yet why? he thought, why? Why? Or rather . . . How? How? It had been just a simple four word question, 'How's life for you?' He thought it was the seriousness of the expression, and the serious look in his eyes and a seriousness of his tone of voice. All three combined made Simnal have an urge to trust this man – momentarily. But it had been there, just an instant, but it had been there. 'Can't complain,' he replied, valuing the exchange, because that was why he was here, that was his brief, part of the Home Office study of such individuals, that they might be recognized and monitored before they became predators, that their methods of controlling and manipulating be analysed, so defended against.

'Travel far?' Again, a concerned note in Sweet's voice, a sincere look with wide pupils, and again, after he had rallied from the false sense of being cared for, Simnal found himself once more sliding back into Sweet's clutches. He paused. There was, he found, a distinct sense of losing control, surrendering it to Sweet. He looked at the man, still young, in his twenties, just, blue-eyed, blond, conventionally handsome, trim of figure . . . just as Ruth had mentioned. Deadly.

'About an hour.'

'York?'

Simnal thought, nice guess, nice try, and repeated his answer, 'About an hour.' As he did so, there was a twitch of frustration; a flash of anger across Sweet's eyes; a momentary, almost imperceptible narrowing of the eyelids. It was a subtle change; so subtle that a layman might have missed it – or a schoolgirl. That was something else to note, Simnal observed, this man's facial expression does not readily betray or show or reveal his thoughts . . . thoughts and facial expression are largely divorced. It lent credibility to the diagnosis of schizophrenia. Simnal pondered Sweet's eyes . . . such a deep blue that they were almost black, and looking into them, he thought, was like looking into two bottomless pits. In his experience, many dangerously mentally ill people had glassy eyes, eyes which allowed no access to their souls at all. Looking into them was not dissimilar to looking into a mirror, not in the sense that one saw one's own image, but in the sense that images were being reflected back at one, as if one's own personality was being rejected. Bottomless eyes were quite different: with bottomless eyes, one's personality was being allowed in, there was no glass wall, but there was the sense that one could travel and travel and travel and still not reach the person's soul. Glassy or bottomless, either, such eyes are the eyes of dangerous persons.

'I'll bet York.' Sweet fixed his eyes on Simnal. 'It's an hour from here . . . about . . . and a guy like you, a professional man, can't see you living anywhere but a university town. So what happened to your marriage?'

Simnal's eyes narrowed. He felt his own facial reaction to the question but couldn't help himself.

'Well, there are some reasons why blokes take their wedding bands off . . . lost, stolen, in the jeweller's for adjustment . . . but it's usually back on within three weeks. This is the third visit . . . no wedding ring, yet the circle round the appropriate finger, that circle of faded skin where the ring was, is still visible. So what happened was recent. So, what was it . . . divorce? Bereavement? A little young to be a widower, though it has been known. Met a woman once who was widowed when she was twenty-two . . . married at nineteen . . . three years' wedded bliss and . . . car accident in case you are wondering . . . out your way in fact, York way . . . on the bypass.'

'Divorce.' Simnal could, momentarily, see no reason why Sweet shouldn't know his marital status but then, instantly, realized Sweet had gained something. Sweet nodded slightly as Simnal answered. There it was again . . . that serious-faced approval that he used to such devastating effect. He could so easily see why a nurse in the hospital had found himself smuggling contraband into the ward for Sweet.

'Recent?'

'As you observe.'

'So what happens in this session?'

'Happens?'

'Well . . . you visit from the outside, not a home-grown psychologist like Dr Day . . . she is a darling, isn't she? You have come from . . . York way . . . to see me and I think only me, no other patient here talks of being interviewed by you. Oh yes, we do talk . . . we do swap notes, compare and contrast . . . yet unlike Dr Day, who asks me to group words together and shows me ink blots and asks me what I see in them . . . or neat ink drawings and asks me what is happening in the picture, you seem to sit and be content to idle the hour away . . . dare say I'm curious.' Sweet spoke with a classless and a near regionless accent, with just a few clipped vowel sounds betraying his north of England roots. 'But I'm all yours. This is better than soaking up daytime television. Much better.'

'So what shall we do?'

'Go down to the pub for a drink?'

Simnal smiled. 'Is that what you want to do?'

'I think so.'

'You realize you won't be doing that again . . . not for a long time . . . if ever?'

'Yes.'

'Does that bother you?'

'Nope.' Sweet smiled. 'I used to enjoy a pub when it was quiet but couldn't ever allow myself to drink.'

'In vino veritas?'

'Yep . . . frightened of shooting my mouth off when I had had too much. I couldn't even allow myself one beer because of the "more-ish" nature of alcohol and before I knew it I'd have sunk eight or ten beers and there . . . I'd be talking about all those murders.' Then he smiled.

'All?' Simnal echoed, feeling his hair begin to stand on end. 'All' was a strange word to describe three murders. It was three too many . . . and such a young age . . . they had no life at all and then Sweet robbed them of what life would have been theirs – but 'all' . . . not just 'those', which would be a more usual way of referring to three murders. Simnal sat back in his chair. A chill shot down his spine, his stomach felt hollow. Sweet's eyes were still bottomless but now there was a sheen to them, and his mouth gave the slightest indication of a smile. 'How many are we talking about, Humphrey?'

Sweet shrugged and instantly Simnal saw the game. It was a game of control. Outside he controlled the taking of life. Outside he had abducted a schoolgirl, held her for a few days and then murdered her and had done that three times. From the moment the abduction was successful, to the moment his victim shuddered as life left her, he, the wholly inappropriately named Humphrey Sweet, had been in total control of her. He was no longer able to do that, not now he was in Kempton with many high walls and locked doors and CCTV cameras betwixt and between him and the outside world, but the urge was the same, the urge being the need to control before finally destroying. It was a classic symptom, Simnal knew that, well documented in the annals of the Dangerous Personality Disordered. Sometimes the need was sexual, sometimes sadistic . . . sometimes it was the need for total control, often it was a mix of all three . . . before the final act of ultimate control: the taking of another person's life on a whim. Now the control had taken on a new form, but it was control nonetheless. Now it was a game of 'I have knowledge but I will only share it with you on my terms'.

'So how many, Humphrey?'

'You know how they found me?'

'Hardly great detective work, as I recall . . . as indeed I read.'

'Sitting in a forest . . . well, a woodland really . . . enjoying the birdsong in the middle of a flowerbed . . . love the scent of flowers . . . just sitting there holding the body of little Mary Grubb. Poor soul, imagine going through life with a name like Grubb . . . well, until she got married.'

'Which opportunity you robbed her of.'

'Dare say people would have got used to it . . . after a while, it's just another surname.'

'So, how many?'

'I strangled her . . . just love that . . . last few moments of life followed by such stillness . . . the green wood, the flowers, the birdsong. I stayed with her all night.'

'So I read.'

'Waited until someone found me. In the event it was a middle-aged woman and her dog . . . I was winning, you see . . . we were winning.'

'We?' Again a bolt of ice shot up and down Simnal's spine.

'I was tired of running, you see, Mr Simnal. I just wanted to be caught . . . and the police were not seeing any of the clues I left them . . . so I stopped running. It was my way of giving myself up.'

'So how many . . . how many victims and how many perpetrators?'

Sweet shrugged. 'Now, that would be telling. Anyway, you are not here to investigate my crimes, that isn't your . . . what's the word? Remit. That's not your remit. As I understand it, you are here to find out what makes me tick. What it was that turned me into a psychopath, a moral degenerate . . . what life changing trauma turned a salesman into a multiple murderer?'

'Amongst other things . . . yes.' Simnal nodded. 'Yes, that was the intention but if other things should come to light . . . then . . . well, then we can't ignore them.'

'We?'

'The authorities.'

'Oh . . . I thought you meant "we" like I mean "we".'
Simnal remained silent but thought, MPD. Then he said,
'There are two others . . .'
'Yes?'
'Been with you a long time?'
'Yes . . . as long as I have been killing.'
'What are their names?'
'Leonard . . . he likes being called Lenny, though.'
'Can I meet Leonard? Would he like to talk to me?'
'He doesn't want to talk to you. And it's "Lenny".'
'Sorry . . . Lenny. I think I would like to talk to him.'
'Well . . . one day.'
'Has Dr Day talked to him? Has she met him?'
'No . . . not yet.'
'Not yet? You think she will?'
'Yes . . . sooner than you will.'
'All right. So who is the other person?'
'Alfred . . . and he likes being called "Alf". Alf and
Lenny . . . we did it together.'
'I see. So a gang of three?'
'Just the three of us.'
'You, Alf and Lenny. Might I meet Alf?'
'No . . . he's like Lenny . . . he keeps himself hidden,
well out of the way. He'll likely meet Dr Day though . . .
Lenny and Alf . . . I think they'll like Dr Day. I think Dr
Day will like them.'
Simnal smiled. 'I am sure she will . . . she's a very nice
lady.'
'You like her too?'
'Yes.' Simnal allowed the conversation to wander. He
was once again aware of Sweet's controlling; his manip-
ulation, but he needed Sweet's co-operation. He needed it
especially since Sweet was beginning to disclose the possibility that he'd taken other lives, other than the three the
police knew about. This was new ground, as was the possibility that Sweet suffered MPD. That fact had never been

reported before to his knowledge, though he would confirm that with Ruth before he left the hospital. 'Yes . . . she's a very pleasant lady.'

'Not happy at home, though.'

'That's not for us to discuss, Humphrey.'

Sweet opened his palm as if a gesture of defeat.

'So . . . there were three of you . . . and you have other victims?'

'Many,' Sweet smiled.

'How many?'

'A few . . . a few.'

Simnal paused. He had talked with patients like Sweet before, he knew the trick was 'easy does it' . . . like reeling in a fish . . . allow a bit of slack . . . then reel in a bit more . . . then a little slack . . . but always ensure you reel in more than you allow slack, and quite soon supper will be writhing on the river bank, or in this case, murder cases or missing persons cases can be closed. 'A few?'

'Yes . . . a few.' Sweet held eye contact with his bottomless pit pupils and allowed a smile to form.

'Well . . . a thousand can be a "few" if the whole is tens of millions. Would you like to put a figure on it?'

'No.'

'Well, single figures? Double figures?'

'Double figures. Just.'

'So ten . . . eleven?'

'Perhaps . . . but that includes the three schoolgirls.'

'So . . . seven or eight others?'

'Possibly. If I am telling you the truth.'

'Yes . . . you could be a fantasist.'

'It's possible. Three girls doesn't give me a lot of street cred in here. I get enough . . . but I'd get more if I had adult victims. The more powerful your victim . . . the more credibility you've got.'

'So I believe.'

'There's a guy in here . . . killed a copper . . . now that

is street cred . . . someone else murdered a family . . . adults and children. Me, three schoolgirls, I'm in the second division in this unit . . . but that's better than the third division . . . the bottom of the pile . . . those that left living victims . . . the rapists who didn't kill. I mean nobody gets out of their way.'

'So you want more street cred?'

'I could use a bit more. No one ever has enough street cred . . . it's the currency in here. I'm going to be here for a long time, I need to make it as comfortable as I can.'

'So we can help each other?'

'Yes.'

'Well, think about it . . . if you want credibility in the eyes of the other patients . . .'

'More credibility. I have credibility. I want more . . . I want all I can get . . . all I am entitled to. There's a couple of guys in here I am expected to get out of the way of . . . I shouldn't be getting out of their way, they should be getting out of mine.'

'All right . . . but the rule's the same. If you want credibility in the eyes of your fellow patients, you've got to have credibility in my eyes.'

'I have?'

'Of course . . . otherwise you're a fantasist. And once you are deemed a fantasist you'll be in division three as you call it . . . amongst the rapists.'

'I'll never be one of them.' Sweet sneered and looked at the floor. 'Never.'

'Well, so far you are a fantasist.'

Sweet shot a glare at Simnal.

'Well, you are.' Simnal pressed his advantage. 'Give me something, anything that will tell me there is substance to your claim of seven or eight other victims. Have all the bodies been discovered?'

'Yes . . . no . . . no . . . there's one . . . one is still missing . . . least I haven't read of him.'

17

'Him?'

'Yes,' Sweet smiled. 'We were . . . we are very versatile, Lenny and Alf and I. Prepubescent schoolgirls are nice . . . but . . . they are a narrow field.'

'Where is his body?'

'If I should die, think only this of me . . .'

'In the corner of a field?'

'Yes.'

'Foreign?'

Sweet shrugged.

'Foreign as in Continental Europe?'

'This is the Night Mail.'

'Scotland?'

Sweet smiled.

'You're getting there.'

'I need more. We need more.'

'What is said about the Lake of Menteith isn't true.'

Simnal furrowed his eyebrows. 'What *is* said about the lake of Menteith?'

'That won't be too difficult to find out, since only one thing is said about the lake.' Sweet stretched and yawned. 'That's enough for today.' He stood and tapped on the pane of glass.

'You mentioned clues?'

'Yes. And I repeated it.'

'When?'

'In our conversation . . . twice in fact. I'm not going to repeat it.' He stood.

David, the nurse, tapped on the door and opened it. 'Finished?' he asked.

'Yes,' Sweet smiled. 'For this session.'

'Multiple Personality Disorder?' Ruth Day raised her eyebrows. 'That's news to me. I'll certainly bear it in mind and enter it . . . well, the possibility of MPD, into his case notes.'

'Two alters that he mentioned,' Simnal relaxed in the chair in front of Ruth's desk, finding it enjoyable to speak to someone who was not dangerously mentally ill and particularly pleasant to talk to. 'One yclept "Leonard" and the other yclept "Alfred", "Lenny" and "Alf" being their preferred titles . . . he didn't let me meet them.'

'Not unusual . . . quite early to expect to meet them. MPDs keep their alters well hidden sometimes . . . as you know . . . and you've made more progress than we have . . . just your third session and you've uncovered MPD. Well done, I'm impressed . . . you clearly "click" with him. On a professional level that is.'

'I was going to say . . . not the sort of person I'd like to "click" with on a personal level.'

'Indeed, but MPD and more victims. This has been a fruitful visit.'

'We'll see . . . I didn't get the impression he was fantasizing . . . he's in for life . . . he knows that he'll never breathe free air again . . . never again will he choose what he wants to eat and when he wants to eat it . . . so his only hope of progress is to increase his victim list and by that means gain more prestige in the eyes of the other patients. So I tend to believe him, but I emphasize "tend". He may be criminally insane, and if so he is appropriately placed in this hospital, but it equally may be the case that he fears a mainstream prison more than he fears life in Kempton. So for the time being I reserve any judgement. I want to retain a healthy scepticism about Mr Sweet.'

'Yes . . . how do you feel?'

'Drained.'

'Yes . . .'

'I had to fight to keep him out of my head.'

'Yes . . . I know what you mean, the approving eye contact, the pleasant looks . . . I mean pleasant appearance . . . he's a handsome devil. Literally.'

'A false knight indeed,' Simnal agreed. 'Those schoolgirls wouldn't have stood a chance . . . he could . . . he would have charmed them into his car, overcoming anything and everything their parents would have warned them about. And that's another reason why I believe him . . . three victims and he gets tired of waiting to be caught?'

'Yes.' Ruth nodded and swept her hand through her hair at the side of her head, revealing her sharp, well-balanced features. 'That is a low number . . . previous studies have shown us that at the third victim the serial killer is getting excited . . . enjoying the feeling of omnipotence . . . but ten or eleven . . . then he'll be tiring, wanting to be caught.'

'Strange the notion of wanting to be caught. Real as it is . . . the way these people deliberately leave clues behind yet can't walk into a police station.'

'Ah . . . but we are in our infancy.' Ruth smiled a warm smile. 'The psychologist who supervised my PhD once said that if the knowledge of the workings of the human mind are represented as a golf ball, then it would not surprise her if the whole knowledge of the working of the human mind would on the same scale be represented as a beach ball. We are just over a hundred years old.'

'I know . . . compared to the medical profession's two thousand year study of the body . . . infancy, as you say. And he mentioned clues . . . he said he mentioned clues in our conversation but nothing seemed out of the ordinary . . . something may occur to me. So what do you think he meant about the Lake of Menteith?'

'I've never heard of it.'

'It's in Scotland. Apart from that, I don't know anything about it.'

Ruth smiled. 'Fancy a cup of tea . . . or coffee?'

'I'd love a cup of tea or coffee . . . especially after that interview. Why?'

'Well, I don't know anything about the Lake of Menteith but I know someone who might. Shall we . . .?'

Ruth Day and Maurice Simnal walked side by side from the DSPD Unit towards other buildings in the hospital grounds on a red gravel path, which snaked through landscaped gardens. As they walked, their bodies once again brushed lightly against each other, and neither objected. Simnal found Sweet's words 'not happy at home' echoing in his brain. Ruth directed Simnal to a doorway over which were the words, blue on yellow, 'Staff Refectory'.

The refectory was quiet at that moment. A few tables were occupied by nursing staff sitting in pairs or individually. The room was bright, airy, modern, with huge sheets of glass on the far wall, which provided relaxing views of the smooth, rolling farmland of East Yorkshire, then a quilt of gold and green under a massive, cloudless blue sky. Ruth walked up to the counter and ordered a tea. She then turned to Simnal. 'What would you like?'

'Tea for me too, please.'

'Two teas, please. Is Sadie around?'

'Aye . . .' The woman poured the teas and at the same time turned and yelled, 'Sadie, pet . . .'

Sadie emerged from behind a rack of trays and walked to the counter. She seemed to Simnal to be a bumbling, rotund woman in her middle years with a ready smile.

'Sadie,' Ruth said warmly.

'Dr Day . . .' Sadie spoke with a strong Scottish accent.

'We . . . me and this gentleman here, we were wondering if you could help us?'

'Aye . . . if I can, hen.'

'It's about the Lake of Menteith.'

'Och aye . . .' Sadie's eyes seemed to light up at the mention of the name. 'It's in the Highlands, hen.'

'What is said about it, Sadie?' Ruth picked up a cup of tea and handed it to Simnal.

'It's Scotland's only lake.'

'Really?'

'Aye . . . all the others are lochs . . . Loch something,

or something Loch . . . but the Lake of Menteith is the only lake in Scotland.'

'No other body of water in Scotland is called lake?' Simnal asked.

'No, pal . . .' Sadie smiled. 'The Lake of Menteith is Scotland's only lake.'

'Nothing special about it?'

'Not that I know of, but then I've been in England these twenty years . . . but I mind when I was a wean in Coatbridge learning about Scotland, the map on the wall in front of the class and the teacher pointing where places were and she said, "That's the Lake of Menteith, it's the only lake in Scotland." That was the first time I heard that . . . then I heard it many times since. Aye . . . it's true. It's the only lake in Scotland.'

'It's not, you know.' Simnal sipped his tea. 'I bet you there's another body of water in Scotland called Lake something . . . and that the Lake of Menteith being Scotland's only lake will be proved to be a widely held but erroneous belief.'

'If Sweet is telling the truth.' They sat at a table by the window. 'Beautiful part of the world.'

'East Yorkshire? Yes, it's very pleasant in the summer. You are not from this area?'

'No . . . London.' She looked down at the tabletop. 'Fulham.'

'Ah . . .'

'Married a man who works up here.' She spoke with a muted tone and Simnal saw that she was indeed unhappy at home. 'Anyway,' she looked up and smiled, 'that doesn't help us with the matter in hand. What will you do now?'

'Report it to the police. I've met the officer who led the investigation into Sweet's murders . . . he'll be the one to inform. If there is another lake in Scotland, the police will know. My guess is that it will be near the border.'

'English influence you mean?'

'Yes. Can't imagine anything north of the Glasgow –

Edinburgh line being called lake . . . but near the English border, and also because Sweet quoted from Auden's "Night Mail" . . . mentioned "border".'

'This is the night mail crossing the border?'

'Yes. The name lake . . . the mention of border . . . and the night mail goes up the west coast mainline through Carlisle and crosses into Dumfries and Galloway. It'll be there . . . if it's there at all . . . just north of the border on the western side of Scotland. I'll put that to Tom.'

'Tom?'

'Tom Mautby, he's the police officer who investigated the murders. He's in York.'

'Nice city. Interesting place.'

'It's a bit like living in a museum, to tell you the truth. That's why we moved out.'

'We?'

'My wife and I.'

'Oh . . . I didn't think you were married . . . sorry.'

'You mean I have that look of a careworn bachelor? That's because I am getting divorced.'

Ruth looked up at him. Once again her pupils dilated.

'Where do you live now?'

'Hutton Cranswick.'

'That's not too far from here.'

'Half an hour's drive. We moved out to settle our son in a village school . . . that was the plan . . . then the marriage went pear-shaped . . . so he got unsettled and went back to York.'

'A son? That's nice. How old is he?'

'Toby . . . he's seven. We share him. Mine every second weekend.' He paused. 'Do you have children?'

'No,' she said with a vigorous shake of her head. 'I don't plan to, either.'

An interesting answer, thought Simnal. But he didn't explore further.

*   *   *

Tom Mautby listened as Simnal recounted his conversation with Humphrey Sweet. Simnal found Mautby to be a gentle, soft-spoken man. He was large, even for a police officer, and that, in Simnal's eyes, made his gentleness all the more appealing.

'Doesn't surprise me.' Mautby sat forward in his chair and rested his elbows on his desktop. He interlaced his meaty fingers and glanced to one side. 'Doesn't surprise me at all. Up to eight more victims . . . still out there . . . now I know why he looked so smug. Now I can understand why he wants us to know what he did . . . now he wants the credit, it won't harm him, he's in for life anyway.'

'I think he was genuine,' Simnal offered.

'Oh, I am sure he was . . . or is . . . felons like to be credited for what they've done if there is no penalty attached to said confession. Even felons that are barking mad, like Sweet.'

Simnal glanced round Mautby's office. It was kept neatly with just a Police Mutual calendar as wall decoration. 'I'll be seeing him again next week,' Simnal said. 'I had thought about increasing the frequency of visits . . . but there seems to be no hurry.'

'No hurry?' Mautby raised a questioning eyebrow.

'Well, if he is telling the truth, all his victims are deceased. If one was being kept alive somewhere . . . that would be different, that would be intense time pressure. So I think I'll keep to my planned weekly appointments. He's a cunning and a manipulative individual. I don't want to play into his hands too much. So for that reason I'll keep the visits to weekly. I can extend the number if I wish. I had originally envisaged twelve sessions. If he starts spilling many beans I'll see him as often as it takes to get the whole story.'

'Thanks . . . and the clue he mentioned?'

'No idea . . . he said he gave me the clue again in our conversation. I'll have to go over that one in my mind.

Well, I'll let you know what he tells me next week. I assume you are still the interested police officer, Tom?'

'For my sins,' Mautby grinned. He was missing a few top teeth, but was clearly not a man to be concerned with false ones. 'I'll transmit what you have told me to the Dumfries and Galloway people, see if they know of a lake in their patch. If it's there, I am sure they'll know of it. It would be like having a "loch" in England . . . it's the sort of thing folk would know . . . would be a local knowledge thing. See what they come up with.'

'Possibly near the railway line.' Simnal stood. 'Just an afterthought . . . his reference to Auden's poem . . . it suggests the proximity to the main west coast line . . . not just near the border, but also near the railway line.'

'I'll suggest that.' Mautby smiled. 'Helps narrow the field.'

Alone, once again, in his office, Tom Mautby pondered Maurice Simnal. He had found Simnal to be pleasantly mannered, well spoken – late thirties, he thought – and felt most pleased by the news that Simnal was taking a fresh look at Humphrey Sweet. It had always been Mautby's conviction that Sweet was one of the icebergs of the human race: intriguing of appearance, and from a distance, possessed of a certain beauty. But he was cold of personality despite a superficial warmth, and was hiding much, much more of himself than he was prepared to reveal. Sweet, in Mautby's cynical, perhaps jaded, police officer's mind, was a man who belonged in prison and not the hotel-like comfort of a hospital. Mautby allowed himself a brief smile, a brief nod of his head. A fresh look at Sweet would be no bad thing.

No bad thing at all.

Simnal walked through York's streets. He thought it would literally narrow the field if the body was indeed in a corner of a field near the railway line. It would mean a long linear search pattern either side of the railway line from the border northwards but encapsulated within the area known as 'the Borders', so if his knowledge of Scottish geography was at all accurate, that would mean from Gretna to Beattock. Probably much nearer Gretna, somewhere near a body of water called Lake something. All the Scottish police had to do was find the lake, if it existed, and release the sniffer dogs. He approached Lendal Bridge, where he paused and began to lean on the parapet. The Ouse, below, had a pleasant blue sheen; a large two-storey vessel was evacuating passengers upon returning from a trip down the river whilst a queue of people waited to take their seats on the boat. A blonde girl about twenty pulled slowly but confidently on the oars of a single scull. Folk walked in groups, in pairs, or as individuals on the path beside the river. A whistle blew from the direction of the Railway Museum. Turning, Simnal pondered the road. Over the bridge, heavy with traffic, open-top tourist buses, horse-drawn carriages and a 'fun bus' with a traction unit designed to evoke a railway engine and trailers designed to evoke railway carriages taking family groups to the Railway Museum, took their places amongst cars and vans and small commercial vehicles. The foot passengers jostled on the pavements at either side of the road surface, dressed in summer clothing of a multitude of colours, many carrying day bags and cameras. He felt gauche, in the way, embarrassed that he presented an obstacle that folk had to negotiate on an already crowded pavement.

'Sorry, we are late.'

Simnal turned. The voice belonged to his wife, who had their son by the hand.

'Just arrived,' Simnal replied, smiling at Toby, then holding eye contact with Jane Simnal née Preston. Their exchanges were now cold, distant, polite but perfunctory. It was, though, preferable in his eyes to the rows and tantrums that had caused so much damage in their home. On one occasion she had destroyed his father's collection of Royal Doulton china. It was not a particularly valuable collection but it was almost all he had to remember his father by, and on another occasion she had chased him out of the kitchen with a carving knife. 'Volatile', he had often thought, was just not the word, though he felt that Toby was utterly safe with her. 'We'll have to arrange another rendezvous, this is too crowded to be a meeting place . . . we are in people's way.'

'Yes.' She handed him a small holdall, which he knew contained Toby's change of clothing for the weekend. 'Will you suggest somewhere?' She was blonde. Casually dressed.

'Yes. I'll think of somewhere.'

'It has to be central.'

'Of course. Though I still have no objection to collecting him from your home . . . and returning him.'

'I have. My neighbours' curtains tend to twitch enough as it is. This is very public but it's also anonymous. I like it that way.'

'Very well . . . perhaps the railway station foyer?'

'That will do. You'll confirm it before Sunday?'

'Yes.'

She turned on her heel and was swallowed by the crowd. Simnal took his son's hand and led him to the car park on Leeman Road and thence to Hutton Cranswick.

It was, for Simnal, an unremarkable but a pleasant weekend's 'access'. He enjoyed Toby's company and was pleased, as any parent would be, that his son was continuing to demonstrate wit and the sort of intellectual prowess that would secure him a university place. They spent a quiet evening together on the Friday, and on the Saturday, drove back into York for the long-promised, and equally enjoyed by father and son, visit to the Railway Museum, and an exploration of the snickelways of the medieval city. The Saturday evening was spent watching television until Simnal senior decided that it was past Simnal junior's bedtime and then he sat alone sipping a whisky and thinking of the days before the 'Big S', as his wife was wont to refer to their separation. The break-up had been awful, the rows had got dangerously close to actual physical violence, but before that, before the rot had set in, the days when he and she sat up in the evening, enjoying each other's company, each other's presence, with Toby asleep upstairs, the days when 'it' was working, were memories to treasure. Now, now the house, even with Toby in it, seemed so empty. It was not, he thought, so bad during the summer, but he found the winters hard, especially the east wind that howled across the flat landscape, biting, icy; it seemed to reach into his very soul. Those winter nights when he was alone in the large erstwhile family home . . . those were the worst. On the Sunday, father and son went for a stroll together along the lanes near their village identifying flowers and trees, and birds and rabbits. After a late lunch and after confirming the new rendezvous, Simnal drove his son to York and rendezvoused with Jane, as suggested, in the foyer of the railway station. Their eyes met briefly. He saw a sadness in her eyes, not before seen so clearly, as if to say, 'I don't like this any more than you do'. Few words were spoken, but there was a profundity of communication which took Simnal by surprise and which he thought about for the remainder of the day and well into that evening.

Tom and Luke Mautby strolled casually along the road with Tom holding Hector on the lead. They entered the Victoria Arms and bought each other pints of beer and a packet of crisps for Hector. It was crowded and smoky in the 'Vicky Arms', with a soft but continuous hum of conversation. After four pints each and to Hector's relief and delight, they walked home; a pleasant Sunday afternoon 'wet' before a home-cooked roast joint.

Father and son.

Two

'Well, our mutual friend is right and he is wrong.' Tom Mautby sat back in his chair with his hands clasped behind his head. It was normally a gesture of relaxation but Simnal saw a clear look of concern, nay worry, in his eyes. 'The upshot is that the boys north of the border have got a result.'

It was not until the following Wednesday that Simnal had heard from Mautby. The Monday and the Tuesday of that week had been routine for Simnal, seeing patients, compiling and filing reports, supervising a PhD student and delivering a lecture at the university. On the Wednesday morning a note in his pigeonhole advised him that DCI Tom Mautby had phoned, and asked him to return the call. Simnal did so and was invited to call round at the police station at his earliest. An unseasonably chill weather front was passing through the Vale of York that day occasioning Simnal to wear a woollen jersey beneath his jacket, which he thought particularly apt. The phone message from Mautby could only mean one thing and it made him shudder. He walked hurriedly from the Dept of Psychology (Home Office) on Bootham, which stood adjacent to the house in which Guy Fawkes was reputed to have been born, to the police station on the Stonebow. When taking a seat in Mautby's office he noticed that the good police officer had also donned a jersey that day. It was after the preliminaries that Mautby said that 'our mutual friend' had been both right and wrong.

'Oh?' Simnal relaxed in his chair. 'That was quick.'

'Not really . . . not if there was a body there. Thanks to you they were able to narrow the field down and then they did what any police force would do and let the sniffer dogs loose.'

'So he was right?'

'Yes . . . which is the worrying thing. What happened was that the police in Dumfries and Galloway pored over maps of their area and asked of local knowledge and couldn't find a body of water called "lake". Plenty of "lochs".'

'But no "lake"?'

'That's right. Anyway, one of them, probably more computer literate, as I believe the term is, had the idea of looking on the web . . . found a site run by the Scottish Office devoted to the geography of Scotland . . . every place name is listed . . . so he typed in "lake".'

'There is another lake?'

'There are many. Well, about half a dozen . . . but . . . but . . . they are all artificially created, they are fisheries stocked with fish where the anglers can go and angle. So Sweet's right in the sense that there is more than one lake in Scotland, but he is wrong in the sense that the Lake of Menteith is still the only naturally forming body of water in Scotland which is called "lake" rather than a "loch".' He paused. 'Anyway . . . the next thing they did was look for a "lake" or a fishery in the Dumfries and Galloway area. In fact they found three, but one . . . one was just inside the border, just north of Gretna and close to the main railway line to Glasgow. So they went there on Saturday morning, let the dogs loose in the corners of the field round the "lake", and got a result pretty well immediately. The problem then was the identity of the remains. They phoned me on Saturday afternoon: remains were that of a young adult male . . . about five foot six . . . small guy . . . recent burial, that is a few years, some remnants of flesh and a zipper and a button with the manufacturer of denim jeans stamped on it . . . so not an ancient corpse. Knowing the reason for our interest and not being able to link the deceased with any of their "mis pers", we trawled ours . . . sent details of a couple of possibilities . . . and yesterday we had to make one of those house calls which we all dread making. It was one of the easy ones, so I was told . . . it was a still strong family unit . . . emotionally speaking. They had long accepted their son as being deceased; he was very good at keeping in touch . . . after four years without a word from him they accepted that he was no longer with us. They are pleased that they can now bury him . . . pleased that the "not knowing" was over.'

'I can imagine,' Simnal nodded. 'As a parent I dread that anything should happen to my son but him disappearing, without knowing what had happened . . . where he was . . . that is my worst fear.'

'As it was mine.' Tom Mautby held eye contact with Simnal. 'My kids are grown up now . . . worried about their own children . . . but parenthood . . . delight and fear all rolled into one. Mind you, I still find myself worrying.'

'Be unnatural if you didn't, Tom.'

'Suppose . . . anyway . . . the young man was a student. Lived in York with his parents . . . studying in London, disappeared one Easter time . . . well, that is Easter four years ago. Took the family dog for a walk one evening, as was the family routine, about ten p.m. Didn't come home. His brother retraced his steps because they always used the same route . . . an hour's hike round suburbia with a bit of wasteland en route where the dog was let off the lead. Anyway, found the dog tied to a fence and no sign of the young boy.'

'Do we know what happened?'

'Nope. No sign of injury on the remains. So, death by strangulation or suffocation would be my guess.'

'Which will be my job to find out?'

'If you can. The young fella's name was Sheenan . . .

Sandy Sheenan. Sweet wouldn't talk to us. He will only talk to you.'

'I'll see where I get. But I won't see him till Friday. I'll keep to the timetable for reasons explained.'

'Well, no hurry. The Dumfries and Galloway police have issued a press release . . . but haven't named him, so media coverage has been confined to Scotland.'

'Thanks. That's something to keep up my sleeve.'

'Just watching, aren't we, Poppet. Just watching the road . . . all the comings, and the goings. Not much else for us to do, is there, Poppet? But there's not much we miss from behind these net curtains, is there, Poppet, I mean, is there?'

Simnal drove from York to Kempton Hospital. He showed his ID at the gate and parked in the visitors' car park. Five minutes later he was sitting in front of Ruth Day's desk. He told her about the body that had been found in Scotland.

'Just as he said,' Ruth sighed, 'this means his claim to have another seven or eight victims . . .'

'Must be taken seriously.' Simnal finished her sentence for her. 'Yes, that significance wasn't lost on me either. Has he said anything to you?'

'Nothing of note. He is being very co-operative, as are all the patients, as I said last week. The staff are working hard to keep on their toes. But really, the patients are running the DSPD unit. We are being especially vigilant during visiting times.'

'Who visits Sweet?'

'Many and varied. Like a lot of patients in here, he has his own fan club. You'd think folk would shun a multiple murderer, especially a child murderer, but people . . . some people, find him fascinating.'

'So I believe.'

'And because they can take the initiative to visit, unlike a prison, wherein the prisoner has to send out a visiting order, all that the hospital requires is a five-day notice of a visit to any patient and if the patient is prepared to receive the visitor then . . . no restrictions. One patient is visited by six members of his family at the same time and the visits take place on the ward, not in a visitors' area as in a prison . . . unless children are visiting, in which case we use the family visiting suite.'

'Have you observed Humphrey Sweet's visitors?'

'I haven't . . . the nurses might have, they are more keen to observe the presence of contraband rather than the visitors themselves. By contraband I mean drugs, of course . . . weapons, any form of pornography, especially child porn in some cases, including Humphrey Sweet . . . to more mild contraband like foodstuffs and tobacco.'

'Might be worth keeping an eye on them.'

'You think?'

'Well . . . given the latest development, he's once again of police interest. Not really our job but it would be public spirited of us. Anyway, shall we go to the ward?'

Ruth stood. 'I'll walk you across.'

Again as they walked through the neatly tended hospital grounds beneath the summer sun, their bodies moved closely, touching occasionally.

In the ward, at the nursing station, Simnal and Ruth Day sat and chatted to David, the charge nurse.

'Nothing to report really.' David sat forward and as he did so, revealed a muscular body and reminded Simnal that because of the nature of patients at Kempton, and hospitals like Kempton, the nurses have to be possessed of physical strength. 'It's quiet, but as we have said in the nursing staff meetings, it's a bit too quiet.'

'I'm glad you're on the ball,' Ruth smiled.

'I too am impressed.' Simnal held eye contact with David who seemed pleased with the recognition of his diligence and of the diligence of his colleagues. Simnal found David to be of pleasant and gentle manner, despite his physical strength, and thus probably well suited to nursing.

'But like I said, it's too quiet. There is the sense that the patients are hatching something.'

'Where is Humphrey Sweet in this, do you think?'

'One of the ringleaders. He has a natural leadership quality about him . . . a dangerous man.'

'Any indication of MPD that you've noticed?'

David pursed his lip. 'MPD? That's new to me with respect to Humphrey Sweet. Confess that would tip the balance, though.'

'Tip the balance?' Simnal raised an eyebrow.

'Well, I am tending to think that Sweet is bad, not mad. I am undecided myself . . . I am not . . . well it isn't my place to make or change any diagnosis . . . that is up to the psychiatrists, but nurses can offer opinion, the day-to-day observations of nurses can influence the diagnosis and, speaking for myself, I am forming the opinion that Humphrey Sweet's diagnosis of suffering insanity is . . . shall we say "generous".'

'Naïve?' Ruth suggested.

'If you like,' David nodded. 'That's perhaps another word which could be used.' David sat back in his chair and in doing so once again, Simnal saw that he moved with a litheness that only superb muscle tone could allow. 'He is deeply manipulative, very self-orientated, is able to control people against their will . . . in fact enjoys control. He is very quick to anger . . . when he doesn't get his own way his eyes narrow.'

'I have seen that,' Simnal said.

'Yes . . . that anger is just below the surface.' David looked at Simnal and nodded. 'Others . . . that is, others on the nursing staff have reported it. He has a low flash point. He is charming, but superficially so, with a low flash point . . . he uses both simultaneously to exert control. He committed crimes . . . the murder of schoolgirls . . . on three separate occasions, which is beyond the comprehension of normal people, but does all that make him insane?' David shrugged his shoulders. 'Is he capable of telling right from wrong? Is he capable of controlling his actions? If the answer to both those questions is "no", then he is insane. But my feelings are tending towards a "yes" answer in both cases.' He glanced out of the window. 'Well, the issue of right and wrong for him might be a bit murky . . . but his leadership qualities, his manipulative streak . . . they are both so strong and well developed that I would say he is capable of foresight, and anyone who is capable of foresight is capable of self-control. So, over the last few weeks, as we approach his six-monthly review, I have found myself tending to the belief that he is sane.'

'Evil?' Simnal suggested. 'I mean, that isn't a diagnosis of course, but within these four walls . . . just to grasp the nettle, that's what we are talking about?'

David smiled. 'Up to a minute ago I would have said "yes", that's what we are talking about . . . he's managed to smooth and charm his way into this holiday camp when he should be in prison paying the penalty he should pay . . . like being carved up in the showers by the other cons . . . but a minute ago you mentioned MPD. If that is the case, well then, he is appropriately placed after all. If that is the case.'

'He mentioned two alters . . . "Lenny" and "Alf".'

'I'll keep an eye . . . and an ear out . . . but he's only ever presented the one personality to me and none of the other nurses have recorded any other personality presenting . . . it's the sort of thing that would not be missed.'

'Dr Simnal asked about his visitors,' Ruth said.

'Yes.' Simnal sat back in his chair, allowing himself to glance out of the window at the gardens, the fence, high and imposing, a road a few hundred yards beyond the fence, fields beyond the road, woodland on the skyline. 'Because there have been developments.'

'Oh?' David showed an alertness, a ready interest.

'Yes . . . sadly . . . you won't have heard of it because it's been confined to the local media in Scotland.' He then told David the discovery of the body of Sandy Sheenan, exactly where Humphrey Sweet said it would be. Simnal watched David's complexion pale and his jaw sag as he related the tale.

After a silence of some seconds. 'So we are talking about other victims . . . quite a few other victims?'

'Yes.'

'Oh . . .' David glanced at Simnal and then at Day and then back to Simnal. 'So this is the beginning . . . this is a can of worms about to be opened?'

'Yes.'

'He's taken to singing or humming that song . . . "Flowers of the Forest".'

'I don't think I know that song. Is it recent? A rock song?'

'No.' David smiled.

'Hardly,' said Simnal, 'it's been around awhile, it's mentioned in the song about a man pondering the grave of a soldier called William McBride, as I recall . . . who was just sixteen when he died . . . "Was it quick and clean or slow and obscene?" being one line I recall. He sings that song as well.'

'That's it.' David smiled. '"Did they beat the drum slowly, did they play the pipe slowly as they lowered you down?", that's the song. He's shown an unusual partiality to it in recent days . . . since you were here last in fact, Dr Simnal . . . often whistling it in the presence of ward staff, especially so.'

'He's telling us something.' Dr Day turned to Simnal. 'It's a clue of some sort. "Lowering down" . . . a grave . . . but he didn't bury the girls . . . "Quick and clean or slow and obscene" . . . but the girls showed no sign of being tortured.'

'Not physically,' Simnal spoke softly, 'but they were held against their will for a day or two . . . that's "slow and obscene".' His eye was caught by the sight of a magpie lighting on the lawn outside the nursing station window. 'One for sorrow,' he said. Then he added, 'What do we know about Sweet's background?'

'Precious little, really,' David said. 'Not very much at all. We have a home address where he lived prior to his arrest . . . but in terms of background . . . very little. It's a strange omission.'

'Who is his next of kin?'

'Parents. Stanley and Doreen Sweet. Out by Selby way.'

'I think I'd like to visit them,' Simnal said. 'Help me get a feel of the man.'

'May I come with you?' Ruth turned to him, her mouth a gentle yet distinct smile of approval.

'Yes.' Simnal felt a rush of excitement. 'Yes. We'll make it a joint visit . . . a two-hander. We'll get our diaries together after I have seen our mutual. I am sure he'll be very pleased when I tell him we have discovered the body of Sandy Sheenan.'

David stood. 'I'll go and get him. But there have been no visitors this last week. Just the police.'

Humphrey Sweet did indeed seem to Simnal to be pleased when he was told of the discovery of the body of Sandy Sheenan. 'Will it be on the national news?'

'Oh yes . . .' Simnal avoided eye contact with Sweet. 'Yes, I think you'll have your day of glory . . . more than one day.'

Sweet beamed. 'Just a day?'

'A period . . . it's the way of it . . . perhaps sadly, but people will hunger for news of your crimes . . . the police will be visiting you.'

'They've been, the bully boys in blue . . . B. B. B. . . . they came here, tried it on, hard cop, soft cop routine . . .

didn't get them anywhere, just refused to talk to them.'

'What about "Lenny"? What about "Alfie"? Did the police want to talk to them? Did they want to talk to the police?'

'They didn't want to talk to the police. The police didn't want to talk to them.' Sweet interlaced his fingers and put his hands behind his head. 'I told the cops I wouldn't talk to anybody but you and Dr Day. If they want information about other victims they get it from you or Dr Day, or both.'

Simnal hesitated. He knew he was treading a difficult line. 'You can't confide in me.'

'Oh . . .' But said with a smile. The smile, Simnal thought, of one who knows very well the game he is playing.

'But you know that. Anything you tell me, I tell the police. Anything you tell me, I tell the staff at the hospital.'

'Including the nurses?'

'Including the nurses.'

Still Sweet smiled. He had power, he had Simnal's attention and he knew it. Simnal knew he knew it, and Sweet knew that Simnal knew that he knew. Of the two of them, Sweet was the one incarcerated, but it was still Sweet who had the power.

'So what did you talk about?'

'Who talk about what?'

'You and David and Dr Day.' Sweet spoke softly. 'Before David collected me, you had a little pow-wow . . . just the three of you, at the nursing station.'

'Yes, we did. We sat in plain view. No denying it.'

'Talk about me?'

'Yes.'

'What did you say?'

'What do you think we said?'

Simnal saw a flash of anger in Sweet's eyes: his response took Simnal by surprise. He remained silent. It was up to Sweet to respond.

'About me?' Sweet said. There was an edge in his voice.
'Yes.'
'What did you say about me?'
'What do you think we said?'
'I don't like people who play games.'
Rich coming from you, Simnal thought, but said, 'I'm
not playing games. This is serious. If you have taken the
victims you say you've taken, this is deadly serious. Also
remember one thing . . . I want information from you.'
'Yes . . .'
'But I'm the one that can leave the hospital. I'm the one
that can enjoy home cooking this evening and stroll out for
a beer or two. You can't.' He eyed Sweet with distaste.
'You like to be in charge, don't you, Humphrey? You like
to call the shots. You get frustrated. Being in here for a
few months, no prospect of free air . . . not ever . . . banged
up with other people like you, all adept at scheming, controlling, manipulating, playing games with other people's
minds, but you can't control other patients as much as you
can control people who can't see through you. Here you
are all alike . . . you may be trying to become one of the
top dogs in this unit . . . but any control you have in here
is nothing compared to the control you had out there . . .
that's why you decided to tell us about your other victims.
But this is a two-way street, Humphrey. I don't think you
are very used to two-way streets . . . if at all. Your life has
always been a one-way street . . . getting your own way.'
 'Until I got fed up waiting to be caught.'
 'Yes . . . because by then you wanted the notoriety . . .
you wanted the reward for murdering all those people, you
said so yourself . . . there's a couple of patients in here that
you think have the edge over you.'
 'Yes.'
 'So if you want the notoriety . . . you have to provide
me with information. So what do you think we said about
you?'

'How to approach me? Was that it . . . hard psychologist, soft psychologist?'

'Nope. In fact we decided to find more out about you . . . more about your background.'

'To see what makes me tick?' Sweet smiled.

Simnal pursed his lips. 'Could say that. Grew up in Selby, I believe?'

'Around there. Nothing remarkable happened to me. Grew up . . . left home.'

'We will be visiting your next of kin.'

Again a narrowing of the eyes, as Sweet seemed to realize there was something beyond his control. 'You will?'

'Yes. We will.'

'Doubt they'll talk to you.'

'We'll see. Relatives most often do want to talk . . . we find that . . . anything to help their kin. Don't you want us to talk to them?'

'No. I don't. I don't want that.'

'Why?' Simnal smiled. 'Do you resent the lack of control?'

'I just don't want you to see my parents . . . I mean, they're getting on now.'

'We'll be . . . sensitive.'

'We?'

'Dr Day and I will visit.'

'She fancies you. I can tell. I watched you walk over here . . . how your bodies touched as you walked . . . how she looks at you. You'd make a nice couple.'

'Tell me about Sandy Sheenan.'

'You found his body very quickly.'

'You gave us all the clues we needed. So tell me about Sandy.'

Sweet smiled. 'Rather think you've taken a shine to her, haven't you?'

'Humphrey,' Simnal growled, 'this is about you . . . and Alfie and Lenny . . . not me. So tell me about Sandy Sheenan.'

'I don't want you visiting my parents.'

'Tough. We are visiting. So, Sandy Sheenan?'

Sweet shot a cold glance at Simnal. 'You talked about more than my background.'

A silence.

'All right . . . yes, we did . . . we talked about your visitors.'

'I get lots of visitors.' Sweet smiled. 'And lots of letters.' He sat back in the chair looking pleased. 'Lots of both.'

'Any favourites?'

'Letter writers or visitors?'

'Either . . . well, let's say visitors. Before we go on to talk about Sandy Sheenan . . . because we are going to talk about him.'

'We are?'

'Yes.' Simnal spoke firmly. 'You see, Humphrey . . . this is a hospital . . . you are here because you have been deemed to be not responsible for your actions . . .'

Sweet smiled. Fatal, thought Simnal, very interesting and fatal. When he saw the smile he instantly tended to the nurse's assessment that Sweet was possibly responsible for his actions. It was short-lived, and Simnal sensed that Sweet regretted showing it. He didn't comment, but the smile was noted. 'But the easier regime at the hospital is only part of the story . . . the other part is that in hospital there is treatment.'

'The therapy in groups and individual sessions?'

'Yes, Dr Day says you've been contributive.'

'I do my best.'

'Well, one of the treatments in the hospital is to encourage patients to depart from a manipulative controlling attitude.'

'You think I am manipulative and controlling?' Sweet's expression hardened.

'Yes. As are all patients in here. It's a common trait amongst patients in this unit.' Simnal paused. 'So you and I will be talking about Sandy Sheenan. Because I say so.'

Sweet glanced at Simnal.

'So we'll be talking to your relatives, and you and I will talk about Sandy Sheenan.'

Sweet shrugged. It was, felt Simnal, the classic attitude of a disingenuous and manipulative personality: if you can't manipulate, don't try.

'So . . . visitors?'

'People find me fascinating.'

'Some people.'

'Some being enough to guarantee personal mail each day. It keeps me going.'

'You feel that . . . the need of contact from the outside to keep you going in here?'

'Yes. Wouldn't you?'

'I dare say. So, anyone in particular?'

'Kathleen . . . I like her . . . she visits me. She visits often.'

'Kathleen what?'

'Why? Are you going to visit her as well?'

'Possibly . . . possibly not. We're trying to take the measure of you, Humphrey. Other folks' perspectives are always interesting.'

'Hood. Kathleen Hood.' Sweet smiled at his mention of the name. 'She's really my type of girl.'

'Really . . . you must look forward to her visits.'

'I do. She's coming tomorrow . . . pity you'll miss her.'

'I will.'

'You don't work on Saturdays . . . or do you?'

'I could make an exception. Anyway . . . Sandy Sheenan?'

'Ah . . . Sandy . . . cried like an infant . . . but he didn't obey the rules, you see, and if you don't obey the rules you face the consequences . . . me and Lenny and Alfie . . . it is our mission to punish those who transgress . . . it is our purpose . . . our fate . . . our destiny.'

'I would still like to meet Alfie and Lenny.'

'In time . . . they are with me . . .'

Simnal thought that the balance had then swung back to an assessment of insanity . . . further reference to his alters . . . their duty . . . their destiny . . . the need to penalize those who transgress. He asked, 'Is this how you selected your victims?'

Sweet nodded. 'It was our purpose, you see. The little girls . . . each wandering along without an adult . . . not just in company . . . not even in sight. That was naughty.'

'And what rule did Sandy Sheenan break?'

'Oh, him . . . Sandy . . . dear Sandy . . . he broke much the same rule, dear boy.'

'But he was an adult.'

'Yes, but even so there are rules to obey . . . when in the city at night . . . stay with the traffic . . . don't take short-cuts down dark streets . . . walk facing the oncoming traffic and what did he do, silly boy, but take a short cut . . .'

'How do you know he was taking a short cut?'

Sweet smiled. 'The dear boy told us.'

'Us?'

'Told me and Alfie . . . Lenny wasn't there.'

'He was easy to overpower . . . just the dog to tie up.'

Simnal shivered. 'Just how many of you . . . physically speaking . . . how many of you overpowered him?'

'Just one . . . physically speaking.'

Simnal felt a sense of relief. 'Oh.'

'Banged over the head, into the back of my car. All over in a few seconds. He was a small youth.'

'How long did you keep him alive?'

'Three days. He was killed at dawn . . . the beginning of the fourth day . . . like the soldiers in the First World War who were shot at dawn. For cowardice.' Sweet smiled.

'Do you think that was right? Many were shell-shocked.'

'That's not an excuse.'

'Good job for you that you didn't live back then.'

'What do you mean?'

'Well, think about it . . . I said not a moment ago that

you are here because you have been deemed to be not responsible for your actions. You have been shown mercy. In 1916 you would have been executed. Is it not possible for you to show similar mercy?'

'But I am right . . . we are right . . . me and Alfie and Lenny are right. It is our duty. We have now been prevented from doing our duty further.'

'I see.' Simnal paused. The pendulum, he thought, swings further towards a diagnosis of insanity. If this is sincere, then Humphrey Sweet is perhaps in the correct institution after all. 'And what is wrong in taking a short cut?'

'Putting yourself at risk, aren't you? Especially at night. Kept him in a lock-up near my house . . . let him have water but food was wasted on him so he went hungry, didn't he? I mean, no point in feeding someone if he's going to die in a few days . . . is there? It was spring . . . about . . . well, you know when it was.'

'How did you kill him?'

'Plastic bag over his head. That's why there are no injuries on his body. Put him in the car . . . covered him with stuff . . . drove north . . . just over the border. Buried him next to a lake.'

'Yes . . . your directions were . . . very clear.' Simnal spoke dryly.

'I left a clue . . . the usual clue but it would have disappeared by now.'

'Are you going to tell us of the clue . . . or is that for us to find out?'

'I've told you . . . you must work it out for yourselves.'

'I'm sure we'll get there.'

Sweet smiled. 'We'll see. We'll see if you get there before I give up the last body. I want my credit . . . I want recognition.'

'You're going to give up another body, I think?'

Sweet nodded. 'Not so much give up . . . now . . . what is that phrase that terrorists use? "Claim responsibility",

46

this time I am going to claim responsibility. This fellow was buried by his family . . . with wreaths upon his grave . . . I attended the service, slipped in at the back. It was well attended . . . I mingled . . . like a professional funeral attender.'

'A what?' Simnal sat forward.

'You surprise me, Dr Simnal.' Sweet smiled a smile that Simnal thought best described as sinister. 'People who go to well-attended funerals because they like to soak up the grief. I mean real weirdos. Anyway, I sat at the back. He was a popular old boy.'

Simnal looked at Sweet. He didn't speak. Just sat and stared.

'That's the way Dr Day makes patients talk. Just looks at them.'

Simnal remained silent.

'Seems to work.' Sweet smiled. 'Does with me anyway.'

Simnal continued to look at him.

'Anyway, the old boy. Put up a struggle . . . he went down fighting . . . blood everywhere . . . his, not mine. Well . . . opened his door to a stranger, didn't he? That was against the rules . . . at night . . . probably thought he was still a super-fit twenty-something Royal Marine. He was a Marine once . . . photographs in his house . . . and at the funeral there were lots of men in black blazers with Royal Marine badges on the breast pocket. He was old and grey . . . stronger than most men of his age . . . he landed a couple of punches on me . . . but he was going down by then. I had a two-pound ball hammer . . . but he broke a rule . . . opened his door to a stranger at night . . . others didn't . . . other old boys and girls . . . they wouldn't have opened their doors to me . . . but he did . . . and he paid the penalty . . . left a clue. The boys in blue didn't see it.'

'But you are not going to tell me what the clue is?'

'I already have, in a sense. You'll fail to impress me if you can't identify it. I presume the boys in blue will still have the crime scene pics?'

'Probably. They tend not to throw things like that away.'

A further period of silence followed during which Simnal held eye contact with Sweet.

'He was one of the early ones . . . about ten years ago . . . winter time . . . up in Driffield. Can't remember the old boy's name . . . lived in a housing complex for the old and greys . . . place called Summer Lodge, that I do remember.'

'Summer Lodge, Driffield. Ten years ago?'

'Yes . . . place, location is right . . . time might be out by a year or two either way.'

'He was called Stamner . . . Edward Horace Stamner.' Tom Mautby replaced the phone. 'Seventy-five years, bludgeoned to death in his pensioner's flat. The police at Driffield know the case well . . . sent shock waves round the town, especially the vulnerable elderly. The Driffield police are sending the crime scene photographs to us by courier . . . we have to try to identify the clue he mentions.'

'It will be biodegradable.' Simnal sat back in the chair, which stood in front of Mautby's desk. 'What did he say? He said that, "It would have disappeared by now" being his words. So the clue, whatever it is, will be temporary in nature . . . something that will disappear over a period of time, measured in years.'

'So, not metallic.' Mautby cupped his hand over his mouth, then removing it he said, 'You know, I am beginning to "see" this fellow. I can see how he kept one step ahead of us. All other serial killers have a distinct MO, same victim profile . . . same method of murder. We connected those two schoolgirls for that reason and he was arrested in possession of the body of the third . . . there was a distinct victim profile there, and both, and subsequently the third, were strangled . . . same MO. But no police force would connect those murders with the disappearance of a young man . . . or of the battering to death of an elderly man in another town. This is unique.'

'In our knowledge.' Simnal shifted his position in the chair. 'It's probably been going on for years . . . it's as old as humanity. Serial killers were only identified as such in the 1970s. Up to then, inward-looking local police forces didn't connect murders in their town with murders in other towns, despite similarities. This is the next type of serial killer to be identified . . . different victim profiles, different MO, but it's the same guy. Sweet will get his notoriety all right and he'll get his own label: "variable serial killer", or something. I might even write a paper on him myself. Submit it to the *Journal of Forensic Psychology*.' Simnal smiled. 'Publish or perish . . . that's the rule. I could do with my name being pushed forward a bit. But the issue is that Sweet is the first known serial killer of this type.'

'Variable.' Mautby glanced out of his window. 'You should use that word . . . claim the credit for it.'

'May do . . . but being the first known doesn't mean he's the first. If we accept the term "variable", then "variable" serial killers have existed as long as humanity itself. It's exactly the same as saying Eileen Wuornos was the first American female serial killer. She wasn't. She was the first known, first identified. Not quite the same thing.'

'Point taken. So where are you going with him?'

'As far as I can. I think he'll take me all the way . . . he wants his fame, as he sees it, or infamy, as we might prefer to see it. He's giving up his victims one by one but myself and Dr Day . . . she's a psychologist at Kempton Hospital.'

'Ah . . .'

'We want to begin now to force the pace a little. We're going to visit his parents and he has a visitor he's keen on, we've asked the ward staff to obtain her address . . . and see if she'll talk to us . . . any insight at all is a help.'

'I see.'

'There's no indication of any other person or persons

being involved, he acted alone when he abducted and murdered Sandy Sheenan . . . and mentions no other person being present when he murdered Edward Stamner, so I tend to the belief that "Lenny" or "Alfie" are alters in his Multiple Personality Disorder condition.'

'Which is something of a relief.' Mautby leaned forward and rested his elbows on his desk. 'The thought that there might be conspirators out there is . . . is . . .'

'Sobering?' Simnal grinned.

'Yes, sobering. Well, we'll look at crime scene photographs of the two schoolgirls he strangled and the crime scene photographs of the murder of Mr Stamner. See if we can see something common in all of them. Something, as you say, biodegradable.'

Simnal stood. 'We're visiting Mr and Mrs Sweet tomorrow.'

'Saturday? Good of you to work on a Saturday.' Mautby beamed at him.

'It's an empty weekend when I don't have Toby. It'll fill the day for me. And Ruth Day seems keen to visit as soon as possible. Never waste enthusiasm. I learned that a long time ago.' Simnal smiled. 'I'll let you know of all developments.'

Three

'**D**o you think you'll be able to help him, sir?'
'Well, he's in hospital.' Maurice Simnal found
himself touched by the Sweets' humility, and faith in the
medical profession.

Simnal and Ruth had rendezvoused in Beverley and had
driven in Ruth's car to the Sweets' home address in Selby.
Ruth was, to Simnal's mind, eagerly talkative during the
journey, constantly glancing at him as she drove. He too
found that he was making more and more frequent eye
contact with her. The conversation was small talk as she
drove her Audi along the flat, narrow roads from Beverley
to Selby, via Market Weighton, of patients, of colleagues
experiences, of training, of previous posts . . . but, noted
Simnal, no mention by either was made of the future. Neither
had firm plans. They crossed the toll bridge over the murky
Wharfe and turned left opposite the Abbey, at the sight of
which Ruth said, 'Impressive,' and to which Simnal replied,
'Yes, very.' Having asked directions of a taxi driver whose
vehicle was stationary at the rank by the department store,
Ruth took a left and then a right into a row of small black-
ened terraced houses, which stood by the railway line. The
Sweet household was number thirty-two, an end terrace,
and like the majority of end terraces, was of a larger floor
plan than the mid terrace houses in order to 'anchor' the
line of buildings.

'Well . . . let's meet they who spawned a monster.' Ruth
inclined her head at Simnal and raised her eyebrows. 'See

51

where he spent his formative years.' She twisted the steering wheel until the crook lock clicked and then wound down her window an inch or two to allow the car to 'breathe' in the heat of the day whilst they were in the Sweet household. 'Better close your eyes as you step out of the car,' she advised, 'the glass in tinted . . . it's a lot brighter outside than it looks.'

'Thanks,' Simnal nodded. 'I wouldn't have thought of that.'

'I learned the hard way.' Again she smiled at him, with warm, brown eyes.

Out of the car Simnal did indeed find the sun fierce in both heat and glare. Ruth's car was evidently air-conditioned as well as having a tinted windscreen and glass. They walked to the door of thirty-two; it was blue with the house number in black plastic and screwed on to the door just above the low-level letterbox. Simnal took hold of the metal knocker and rapped it twice.

'Quite imperious.' Ruth spoke amiably.

'Didn't mean it to sound so,' Simnal replied. 'Don't want to be intimidating.'

'Indeed.'

Any further conversation between them was halted by the opening of the door. A late middle-aged lady stood on the threshold; she had evidently made efforts to look her best for the doctors. The house too, even from the street, smelled strongly of furniture polish and air freshener.

'Mrs Sweet?' Maurice Simnal asked.

'Yes, sir.'

'I'm Dr Simnal, this is Dr Day. We spoke on the phone.'

'Yes, sir. Thank you for coming to see us. Mr Sweet is grateful that you can spend time to visit us. It's to help Humphrey?'

'Yes,' Simnal smiled, 'that's why we're here.'

'Yes . . .' Ruth echoed. 'We're all on the same side.'

'Thank you. Please come in.' Mrs Sweet stood on one

side and allowed Day and Simnal to step over the threshold and enter the narrow corridor. 'Please go through to the back room.'

Day led Simnal into the room at the back of the house. Mr Sweet stood in the room in front of the fireplace. He was of similar age to Mrs Sweet but more slender. He was dressed in wide, baggy flannels, which were, thought Simnal, probably fashionable when he was in his prime, a collarless white shirt, the sleeves of which were rolled up military-style, cuff over cuff. He wore carpet slippers on his feet. Simnal noted a thin face, cleanly shaven as if he had not just 'scraped' that morning but had also shaved perhaps less than an hour previously in anticipation of the 'doctors' visit. He was bald, save for a little hair, grey and neatly trimmed, which ran above his ears round the back of his head.

'Mr Sweet.' Simnal extended his hand. Ruth did likewise.

'Yes, sir.' Sweet bowed his head as he deferentially shook Simnal's and Ruth's hands.

'Dr Simnal, Dr Day.' They introduced themselves to him.

'Please, sir, madam . . . please sit down. Would you care for a cup of tea?'

'Yes . . . thank you.' Simnal smiled. Ruth too said she would appreciate a cup. It was one of those situations wherein both Simnal and Ruth sat side by side on a narrow, two-person settee, which, like Mr Sweet's trousers, was of an earlier era. From the settee they looked out across the room to the rear window, which, for some reason, had net curtains draped over it. Simnal could not see the point of having net curtains, or 'sheers' as a Canadian acquaintance referred to them, over the window, because beyond was a concrete yard, and beyond that was a high stone wall behind which, at that moment, a train rumbled loudly and slowly by.

'Goods train,' Mr Sweet said, 'going in that direction,'

he pointed to the wall behind him, 'full of coal. On its way to the power station. We've been here nearly fifty years . . . we have got used to the railway.' He fell silent as the train rumbled past. 'Stops conversation,' he said, 'but we are used to that as well.'

Moments later Mrs Sweet entered the room carrying a tray of tea and a plate of chocolate biscuits that she placed on a coffee table. When tea had been poured, and each person was served, holding a cup and saucer, Mr Sweet said, 'Do you think you'll be able to help him, sir?'

'Well, he is in hospital.' Simnal paused. 'The purpose of all hospitals is the same, that is, to cure if we can.'

'If you can?' Mr Sweet paused. 'Our Humphrey did terrible things . . . those three girls . . . we had friends in this street, and now no one will talk to us. We have had things I can't describe put through our letterbox . . . but Humphrey was ill, no sane person would do that. So if you can cure him, sir . . . and miss . . . if you can.'

'He'll be released then, will he?' Mrs Sweet sat in the vacant armchair. 'I mean, if you can cure him, he'll be let go? He can come back home . . . if he's not ill any more. It stands to reason.'

'It doesn't quite work like that,' Simnal spoke softly, 'but it's not up to myself and Dr Day here . . . we are just a small part of a larger team.'

'And if you can't cure him . . . he stays at Kempton?'

'Yes. I'm afraid so.'

'But you know he's ill . . . not bad. I mean that last little lass he killed, he just sat there holding her body. I mean if he was a bad lad, he'd have run away, wouldn't he?'

'I suppose.'

'So he's ill . . . you'll do what you can to cure him?'

'Yes.' Simnal smiled as he sipped the cooling tea. Disappointingly, it had not been allowed to infuse in the pot and so had a weak taste not dissimilar, he thought, to hot water. 'We are psychologists, not medical doctors, but it does seem to all concerned that what is wrong with Humphrey to make him ill, is in his mind.'

'Yes . . . we understand that.' Stanley Sweet glanced out of the window at the wall beyond the yard. 'I mean, that's why he's in Kempton. I remember hearing about Kempton when I was a lad in the streets . . . had that ring to it, like Broadmoor . . . Rampton . . . and what's that one in Scotland called?'

'Carstairs.'

'Aye, that's it. Used to see it from the train. I remember showing it to Humphrey when he was about ten. We were going on holiday to Scotland to visit my brother. He lives in Glasgow. He married a Scots girl . . . she wouldn't leave Scotland so he left England, but that's our family. Accommodating. Very accommodating.'

'Accommodating,' Doreen Sweet repeated. 'Very accommodating family, the Sweets. I learned that.'

'Aye.' Stanley Sweet raised and lowered himself on his toes. 'You get what you give.' He paused. 'Any road . . . pointed out Carstairs to Humphrey and he just stared at it. It held some fascination for him. Never thought I'd see the day when any son of mine would be in one as a patient.'

'Never see the day.' Doreen Sweet looked down at the carpet, worn, threadbare.

'That's quite interesting, though.' Simnal took another sip of the tasteless tea and thought of Sweet's choice of location for the burial of Sandy Sheenan. A little more seemed to be explained, another piece of the puzzle slotted into place. 'You see, this is what we have come to talk about . . . Humphrey as a boy . . . as a youth . . . whatever you can tell us, it will help us to help him.'

'Now I know why you called on a Saturday.' Stanley Sweet grinned. 'Not the sort of conversation you can have in a normal working day when you've got folk to see. Well, what can we say, mother?'

55

'Where can we start?' Doreen Sweet looked up reverentially at her husband.

'Well . . .' Simnal finished his tea and placed the cup and saucer on the coffee table. 'Did he have many friends . . . or was he a loner?'

'He had friends and he had enemies . . . came home with a bloody nose on more than one occasion. No one ever called on him. When I did see him he was playing with younger children . . . bossing them about.'

'Making them stand in a line,' Doreen Sweet added. 'It was when he tried that with the boys of his age that he got a bloody nose.'

'He was an only child?'

'Yes.' Stanley Sweet spoke firmly. 'When I saw what I put Mrs Sweet through, I said I'd never do that to her again. So I didn't.'

'It was a forceps delivery,' Mrs Sweet explained.

'I see.' Ruth smiled at her.

'You any children, Dr Day?'

'No.' Ruth looked sheepish. 'Not yet.'

'Well I hope things go better for you than they did for me.'

'If they do,' Ruth smiled, 'but thanks anyway. So he had younger friends. What was he like in the house?'

'He liked his own way . . . liked things his way . . . made us swap bedrooms.'

'He did what?'

'Well, originally he was in the back but he kept complaining about the noise from the trains and we thought, well, he needs his sleep for school in the morning and so we agreed to swap rooms even though there wasn't much room for me and Mrs Sweet in the back room. It's a smaller room than the front room, you see.'

'But it was what Humphrey wanted.'

'And we let him grow up alone too,' Mrs Sweet added. 'We did that for him.'

'Aye, we did.'

'What do you mean?' asked Ruth Day.

'Well, despite what Mr Sweet just said about not making me pregnant again, I said I'd go through it again if Humphrey wanted a little brother or sister and Mr Sweet agreed. So when Humphrey was about five we asked him if he wanted a little brother or sister or would he prefer to grow up alone. He asked if he could think about it and two days later he said he'd prefer to grow up alone.'

'So we didn't have any more children,' Stanley Sweet said. 'We did that for him. Did everything for our Humphrey.'

Simnal and Day glanced at each other, aghast. If the Sweets saw their visitors' reaction to their disclosure, they didn't react.

'Bought him a kitten, though . . . from the market. A little black kitten.'

'What was it called?'

'Pitch.' Mrs Sweet smiled. 'It was black you see, like pitch.'

'Ran off,' Stanley Sweet grumbled. 'Just when it had settled . . . it knew where it lived and all that . . . just went out and never came back.'

'Really?' Simnal was not a 'cat person' but knew enough to know that such behaviour was unusual for felines.

'Yes, just wandered as cats will do.' Stanley Sweet rocked on his heels as another train rumbled into Selby station. 'Passenger train,' he said. 'Not as loud as the goods trains.'

'And they always stop,' Mrs Sweet added. 'The goods trains sometimes go straight through . . . and sometimes they stop because of the signals, but the passenger trains always stop. So people can get on and off,' she added help-fully. 'Funny about Pitch though, always wondered where she ended up. No reason to run away from this house so it must have been somewhere fancy. Probably found another cat.'

'Was Humphrey upset about Pitch vanishing?' Simnal asked.

Stanley and Doreen Sweet glanced at each other. 'No, he wasn't.'

Stanley Sweet spoke for both of them. 'No, he wasn't upset at all. He was about ten . . . younger . . .'

'Eight . . . seven or eight.' Doreen Sweet smiled. 'Nice lad he was, lovely little boy.'

'Aye . . . mature beyond his years.' Stanley Sweet also smiled. 'Any other lad his age would be full of tears at the loss of Pitch but he just picked up the cat litter as calm as you please and put it out for the bin men and put the tins of cat food we had left over and put them in the waste bin . . . very mature, I thought.'

'Aye . . . he was like that.' Doreen Sweet continued to smile. 'Funny he went so unwell in life later on.'

'Then there was the rabbit . . . a lop-eared rabbit. We got that after Pitch went missing. My brother in Scotland says it wasn't good that Humphrey should grow up alone, that's why we got the cat and the rabbit.'

'And the goldfish,' Doreen Sweet put in.

'Aye . . . there's a mystery. The rabbit and the fish.' Stanley Sweet pondered the ceiling and paused as the passenger train rumbled out of the station. 'The rabbit . . . that went one night . . . not so much a mystery . . . you can get into those backyards by the alley a few doors down. We kept the rabbit in a hutch at the back and one day Mrs Sweet came home and found that someone had got into the alley, into our yard and stolen the rabbit. Flopsy, we called him. Just opened the hutch and let him out . . . never knew what happened, thought it must have been them animal rights activists who objected to a rabbit being kept in a hutch.'

'See, at about the time them animal rights people raided a mink farm near here and let all the mink out of the cages and they escaped into the wild and we thought they'd done the same to Flopsy.' Doreen Sweet sat back in her chair. 'Well, I suppose it's not good for a rabbit to be kept in a little hutch like that, but if it was done so a little lad wouldn't grow up alone . . .'

'How did Humphrey react to Flopsy's disappearance?' Ruth asked.

'Bit like he did to Pitch really . . . not upset . . . helped Mr Sweet chop the hutch up in fact.'

'Where was Humphrey when Flopsy was taken from the hutch?'

'Where was Humphrey? Out . . . it was a Saturday . . . came back from town with my shopping. Humphrey was out, saw him in the street with his little pals . . . made a cup of tea . . . went out into the yard to put the tea-leaves from the last pot down the drain and saw the hutch door open . . . so Humphrey was out with his pals. Lovely summer's day it was . . . like today. Just like today.'

'Goldfish . . . that's still a mystery.' Stanley Sweet again rocked on his heels. 'Had a goldfish bowl . . . one day it had gone, just disappeared. I mean the bowl was there with the water in it but the fish had gone.'

'Explain that,' Mrs Sweet spoke with a note of triumph. 'As Mr Sweet said, the water was still in the bowl . . . bowl still sat on top of the television . . . but where was Goldie?'

'What takes fish from water?' Stanley Sweet asked Simnal, then Ruth. 'Eh . . . tell me that . . . cats and birds . . . didn't have a cat then and no bird has ever been in this house. Mrs Sweet has a bad chest and birds in cages set her off.'

'Can't go to where they keep birds in a cage.' Doreen Sweet placed her hand on her chest. 'I can't breathe right . . .'

'So that's a real mystery, what happened to Goldie.'

There was a pause, a lull in the conversation. It was broken when Simnal asked what Humphrey Sweet had been like as a teenager.

'He was all right . . . if he got what he wanted we had enough peace in this house.'

'I see. Did he have friends as a teenager?'

'Didn't seem to . . . seemed to be a bit of a loner.'

'Didn't seem to mind, though,' Mrs Sweet added. 'Came home from school, had his tea on his lap in front of the television . . . did any homework he had to do. Stayed in mostly in the evenings . . . at weekends he used to go out by himself . . . or sit on the river bank . . . saw him sitting on the river bank during the summer.'

'No friends?'

'Not to speak of . . . not when he was a teenager. He could play with six- and seven-year-olds when he was ten or so . . . but he couldn't play with ten- or eleven-year-olds when he was fifteen. He didn't want to, anyway.'

'Was he sporty?'

'Good at sports you mean?'

'Yes . . . particularly team sports.'

'No,' Stanley Sweet shook his head, 'wouldn't say that . . . needed football boots for school but he never played in a team. Mind you, I never did . . . Mrs Sweet didn't either, we are just not sporty. This family . . . we make our contribution in other ways.'

'In other ways.' Again the echo from Doreen Sweet. 'We are a good family despite our Humphrey's illness.'

'He's in hospital . . . not prison . . . that tells us a lot.'

'He can't help what he did.'

'Can't help it,' said Stanley Sweet. 'The lad's ill.'

'So he left school . . . any qualifications?'

'None.'

'So what happened?'

'Ah . . .' Stanley Sweet smiled. 'Then he shone . . . our lad . . . then he shone. Really shone.'

'Who needs qualifications?' Doreen Sweet also smiled. 'What Humphrey did after school was . . . we're right proud. Work-wise that is . . . we are proud of what he did work-wise . . . until his illness set in. We are not proud of that . . . but he's ill.'

'Can't help that. Not his fault,' Stanley Sweet growled. 'But what he did for his money . . . now that's a tale in itself. You tell them, mother.'

'He was a salesman.' She brimmed with pride. 'He was a natural . . . just took to the job like a duck to water . . . just sold stuff. Started out at sixteen as a door-to-door boy . . . did well. Got his driving test when he was seventeen . . .'

'Just,' Stanley Sweet grunted. 'Wasn't happy with that . . . I thought he was too young to be behind the wheel of a car. But he got it . . . just.'

'Just?' asked Simnal, who had taken a determined four attempts to obtain his driving licence. 'I thought it was just a question of pass or fail.'

'Well, I'm telling you what Humphrey said when he came home waving that bit of paper . . . driving test examiner said that it wasn't a good pass and he wanted to fail him but he couldn't for some reason . . . so pass it was.'

Simnal and Ruth exchanged a knowing glance.

'Anyway, then . . . once he had a driving licence he got a job selling cars. New cars . . . working for a dealer . . . not second-hand cars.'

'Did a bit of selling trade-ins that the dealer took in part exchange, but he mostly sold new,' Stanley Sweet explained. 'Did well . . . started out with a Japanese dealership selling Nissans and Datsuns . . . then he moved up the ladder as he saw it. When he was arrested he was working for Cohen's . . . you'll have heard of them.'

'Yes,' Day said. 'I bought my car from them. They sell German cars. Well, Mercedes Benz, BMW and Audi . . . they seem to turn their noses up at VW.'

'That's them . . . outlets all over East Yorks and North Humberside. He worked for them for a few years . . . then he got arrested.'

'He was ill,' Mrs Sweet repeated. 'No one sane would do that.' She paused. 'But what a salesman . . . he could sell . . . what's that expression, father?'

'Ice cream to an Eskimo.' Stanley Sweet looked down at the carpet. 'Aye, ice cream to an Eskimo. He just had that knack . . . did well . . . bought himself a Mercedes. Imagine a street like this and a Mercedes parked in it. In this street you're lucky to have a car, let alone a Mercedes.'

'He never left home?'

'No . . . why should he? He was comfortable here.' Mrs Sweet smiled. 'He liked his mum's cooking. No reason to leave home.'

'No lady friends?'

'A few . . . couldn't find "the one", though . . . none of them seemed to last . . . funny that. Not a bad looking boy . . . plenty of money, a good future . . . just could never keep a girl long enough to get near marriage.'

'Any male friends?'

'Not that we knew of . . . did he, mother?'

'Not that we knew of.' Doreen Sweet shook her head. 'He went out at night, stayed out late . . . all night sometimes, but never brought any friends home. Talked about his friends though . . . told us about "Lenny", someone called "Lenny" and another friend . . . what was his name?'

'Alfred.' Stanley Sweet glanced at his watch. 'Told us about Alfred.'

'When did he first mention those two friends?' Simnal asked.

'Oh . . . about . . . four, five years before he was arrested. Wouldn't you say, mother?'

'About that.'

Simnal paused and then asked, 'Did you ever notice any change in his behaviour . . . any "side" to him that was normally hidden?'

'As though he became a different person for a while,' Ruth explained. 'Not a long while . . . a few minutes perhaps?'

'Can't say I ever did.' Stanley Sweet shook his head slowly. 'What about you, mother?'

'I never saw anything like that.' Doreen Sweet also shook her head. 'No . . . never . . . he was always Humphrey . . . never anything but Humphrey. So long as he was happy, things were all right.'

'If he wasn't happy?'

'He had a temper . . . so we kept him happy. Never took any money off him for his keep. Never did. Kept him happy that way.'

'I see . . . I see.' Simnal felt the home visit to the Sweets drawing to a close. 'Do you know of anybody else who might be able to help us get a grasp of what Humphrey was like when he was growing up?'

'Just Mrs Featherstone.'

'Mrs Featherstone?' Ruth asked.

'His school teacher . . . one of them . . . at the secondary school. She's retired now but still has her wits about her. She's a very kind lady. I am sure she'll be happy to help you.'

'Where does she live?'

'Close by . . . go back to the Abbey . . . turn left . . . keep on the main road . . . large yellow painted house set back from the road on the right-hand side.'

Driving away from the Sweets' house, Ruth said, 'Well, the cat and the rabbit will be in a weighted sack at the bottom of the Wharfe and the fish will have gone down the nearest drain.'

Simnal nodded. 'Yes,' he said, 'oh, yes.'

Mrs Featherstone's house was where Stanley Sweet had described.

'Don't like cold calling.' Ruth parked the car at the kerb on the opposite side of the road to where Mrs Featherstone's house stood. 'But since we are here . . .'

'Yes,' Simnal unclipped his seat belt, 'we'll be very polite, very apologetic and hope she doesn't say no.'

After the preliminaries, after identities had been checked, after reason for calling unexpectedly been explained, Mrs Joyce Featherstone invited Simnal and Ruth into her home.

'It is no trouble to talk about Humphrey Sweet.' Joyce Featherstone impressed Simnal as a prim and proper lady, haughty bearing, neatly cut grey hair and wearing a yellow dress with black shoes. The living room of her house was well kept, nothing out of place, but had a preponderance of yellow, dazzlingly so, to Simnal's mind. Yellow vases on the windowsill, a dark coloured carpet with yellow twirls in the pattern, a yellow-tinged painting on the blue wallpaper. The yellow of her dress, the yellow of the exterior of the house. 'In fact, I am surprised no one has ask me beforehand. The evil in people often shows itself when they are children. I taught him between eleven and sixteen. I saw it emerge.'

'You think he's evil?' Simnal smiled. He found he could imagine Joyce Featherstone as a teacher, one of the old school, standing no nonsense, getting results. 'He's in hospital.'

'Kempton,' she sniffed. 'Yes, I know. And yes, I think he's evil . . . he has pulled the wool over your eyes . . . let me tell you. The man is evil.'

'Perhaps . . . but the administration has to be benign in its judgement.'

'Well, he was evil when he was at school. I really am surprised no one has asked me or any of my colleagues, all retired now . . . or deceased, sadly; but none of us were asked for any background on the man . . . not even journalists hungry for a salacious story.'

'Well . . . we can't answer for that.' Simnal relaxed into the deep armchair in which he sat. 'And we are really only here on a whim, otherwise we would have phoned or written in advance. So, thank you for seeing us.'

'It's good of you.' Ruth smiled at Joyce Featherstone.

'A whim?'

'On Mr Sweet's suggestion really . . . we have just visited Humphrey's parents.'

'I see.' She shuddered. 'The use of his Christian name implies approval . . . but I dare say that's unavoidable.'

'You say you saw what you describe as his "evil" emerge?' Simnal pushed the conversation forward. He was beginning to doubt any value of Mrs Featherstone's contribution, she had by then made her dislike of Humphrey Sweet all too clear. He was nonetheless prepared to listen.

'Yes. A very unpleasant aspect of his personality began to develop when he was about fourteen or fifteen. A lot of teenagers go through an unpleasant phase but Humphrey Sweet's unpleasant phase was a lot more unpleasant than most and he didn't emerge from it. He was still unpleasant when he left school.'

'As in?'

'Well, a look began to develop in his eyes . . . a very supercilious look . . . as though the world was beneath him. There was no reason for such aloofness . . . he wasn't a good scholar . . . he wasn't particularly popular. That was the first indication that something was wrong with him . . . other staff reported it too. Then he began to push the envelope of acceptable behaviour, but did so in a very intelligent way . . . he was happy to have suspicion hanging over him, like a permanent cloud, but never allowed proof of his wrongdoing to be evident. That he could cope with being disliked and suspected was part of his haughty nature. It was as if he had taken on board the concept of the burden of proof before he learned the term. Once I witnessed him being shouted at by five male members of staff who were trying to break him into confessing to something which they knew he was guilty of and he just stood there not showing any reaction at all. He told me later that he was thinking of Mount Everest and letting all the harsh words just wash over him. So I said, "So you did do it?" and he winked at me . . . you see, letting me know he'd done it but not confessing as such . . . clever, detached little . . . Sorry, I will not swear but you know what I mean . . .'

'Yes . . . I think I can understand what you are saying,' Simnal nodded. 'I get the gist.'

'I make no secret of the fact that I dislike Humphrey Sweet.' Joyce Featherstone spoke sharply. 'I make no secret of it at all.'

'Appreciated.'

'I was so relieved when he left. Seemed to do very well, which impressed us all . . . a car salesman. Confess I thought he'd be a criminal. I suppose he is now in a sense . . . criminally insane . . . but I thought he'd brush with the law as soon as he left school. But he avoided that . . . too clever by half, if you ask me. It seemed that he sensed that once he left school he was in a different league . . . he sensed that what protection he had at school as a juvenile . . . he didn't enjoy as an adolescent in the community.'

'How did you find his parents?'

'Much as you have just found them, I would think, weak and indulgent. As if they felt they had been given nothing in life and were determined to compensate by giving their one and only everything he wanted.'

'How was he among his peers?'

'From what I was able to observe, he was a very interesting paradox . . . he seemed to struggle for acceptance by his year group . . . he was not well liked or at all popular as I recall, and yet he was always at the centre of things when there was trouble, as if despite being unpopular, he could still manage to be the ringleader. He would often emerge as the leader and boys who would not normally misbehave, did misbehave when following Sweet's influence . . . and misbehave is mild . . . we are talking acts of criminal damage . . . very serious offences . . . but getting hold of him . . . it was as though he was covered in soap, he'd slip through anything. I was his teacher. I feel that I have been contaminated by him . . . heaven knows what he did to his classmates.' She paused. 'Then there is the other side to him . . . this probably more sinister.'

'Oh?'

'Well . . .' Joyce Featherstone inclined her head to one side then straightened it. 'He had this knack . . . I never experienced it but other members of staff reported that they found themselves confiding in him. Remarkable as it may sound, members of staff said they were telling him about their marriage difficulties, their financial stress . . . or their plans for career advancement, then suddenly would think, "What am I doing? What am I saying to this pupil?" Remarkable . . . and these conversations would take place in the schoolyard at midday break, or when walking down the corridor. Imagine a member of staff and a fourteen- or fifteen-year-old having that sort of conversation . . . and these were weighty members of staff, too . . . staff that had no difficulty with class control . . . who commanded respect.'

'Astounding,' Simnal said, 'but I can understand it . . . having met Humphrey Sweet on a few occasions.'

'You are working with him?'

'Yes . . . I am employed by the Home Office,' Simnal explained. 'I have a brief to try to determine what makes Humphrey Sweet and people like him tick. I see him weekly but there have been developments in his case which have . . . not put us under pressure but have, shall we say, increased momentum, which has led to unplanned home visits on a Saturday.'

'I was going to ask if Saturday working was the norm for you.' Joyce Featherstone smiled approvingly.

'And I work at the hospital,' Ruth added. 'I'm employed by the local health authority. I see Mr Sweet twice a week . . . once in a private session, once as a member of a group.'

'I see. So he is being treated. That is good . . . I, like many other laypersons, have the impression that a psychiatric hospital is a softer bed than prison . . . but work is done with the patients.'

'Oh yes.' Ruth smiled. 'As we have explained to the patients, it is a hospital . . . they are there to be cured if possible.'

'If possible.' Joyce Featherstone repeated the words. 'Do you think you can cure Humphrey Sweet?'

'We'll try. Or prove him sane. Or fail to do either. So, one of three options in his case. In any case really . . . in every case . . . each patient at Kempton, especially those in the DSPD.'

'DSPD?' Joyce Featherstone raised an enquiring eyebrow.

'The Dangerous and Severe Personality Disorder Unit,' Ruth Day explained. 'Sorry, just used to referring to it as the DSPD. Well, in the case of every patient, the outcome will be one of three . . . insane, but treatable . . . sane and mistakenly placed in hospital . . . insane and untreatable. We review all patients regularly. At present Mr Sweet is being assessed. It is presumed he's insane but whether that is the case or whether he's wangled himself a place in what you describe as the soft bed . . . but is in fact sane . . . that remains to be seen. He certainly is possessed of enough of a grasp of reality that he is frightened of being sent to prison. But that in itself doesn't mean to say he's sane. He can have that level of awareness and still be barking mad.'

'It's a narrow line, isn't it?' Mrs Featherstone addressed Simnal.

'What is?'

'The line that divides evil from insanity.'

'Strange one that one, Poppet. Always thought so. Keep a good eye on her we will, Poppet, a very good eye. Watch her more than any other . . . right opposite us as well. Makes things easier, Poppet. Makes things a lot easier.'

*   *   *

Maurice Simnal and Ruth Day lunched at the Abbey Café in Selby. They sat opposite each other at a table in the window. An observer might take them for man and wife, both being of the same age group, and both leaning forward being evidently very comfortable in each other's company.

'So what is your situation, Maurice?'

'Situation?'

'Divorced, separated . . .'

'Separated . . . divorce pending.'

'I'm sorry.'

'So am I in a sense . . . who isn't sorry that their marriage ended in divorce, but it's the old story . . . one door closes . . . another opens . . . and it's better for Toby.'

'Your son?'

'Yes.' Simnal opened his wallet and took out a colour print of a smiling, blond-haired boy. 'Here he is.'

'He's lovely,' Ruth smiled.

'Yes, he is . . . he's the reason for everything. He gives so much . . . he's a very giving child.'

She handed the photograph back to Simnal. 'What happened?'

He glanced at her as he slid the photograph back into his wallet.

'Sorry . . . I didn't mean to pry.' She looked sheepish.

'No . . . no . . . it's all right . . . the mistake was mine. I was indiscreet . . . our marriage was going through an arid patch, everything seemed very staid . . . the magic had gone . . . and a student threw herself at me.'

'A student?'

'A PhD student . . . twenty-three, twenty-four . . . not a child. One thing led to another and I was unfaithful for a few months . . . it was already fizzling out when Jane found out. She stormed out, taking Toby with her. Divorce is pending.'

'She won't take you back?'

'Nope.'

'Would you want to go back?'

'I'm not sure.' He glanced up at her just in time to see the briefest of smiles fade from her lips. He knew then that Ruth and he would soon, very soon, become 'an item'. He decided to be diplomatic. 'If we did get back together, it wouldn't be the same. There would always be that sense of contamination and she'd always have my infidelity to hold over me . . . not sure I could live like that.' It was, he thought, at least a half truth . . . the full truth being that he longed, yearned to be able to turn back the clock to the time that Miss Clark started making eyes at him in their Thursday morning supervision sessions, heart-stoppingly beautiful as she may have been, wished he had never accepted her invitation to the party she was throwing with her housemates, wished he had said 'no' when she pressed against him at the party and said, 'Let's stop playing games. We can't go to your house . . . so my room it has to be.'

'That I can understand.' She kept her eyes downcast. 'I couldn't live like that, it would be like walking on broken glass all the time . . . very uncomfortable. But at least you have experienced happiness in marriage.'

'You haven't?' He glanced out of the window as a drab green refuse lorry rumbled by.

'No . . . well, hardly. Meet Mrs Bashir.'

'Bashir?' Simnal furrowed his eyebrows. 'Not Day?'

'Day is my maiden name. I am married to one Dr Abdul Bashir . . . late of Cairo, now of Beverley.'

'You live in Beverley?'

'Yes. Which is why it was very convenient for me to pick you up this forenoon.'

'We are neighbours.'

'Yes.' She smiled. 'Just one stop between Beverley and Hutton Cranswick by train . . . but I'd drive anyway.'

They held eye contact as a profound silence developed between them. Simnal heard echoes of the young Miss Clark except now he expected to hear 'Let's stop playing games.

We can't go to my house so it's got to be yours.' He said, 'Why don't you use your married name?'

'Why advertise my mistake?'

'You have recently come to think that way?'

'Yes.'

'Otherwise you would still be married?'

'Very astute.'

'Very obvious, I would have thought. So what's going wrong? Dare say it's my turn to say "Sorry. I don't mean to pry".'

'From his point of view it's all on track, all going like clockwork.'

'So . . .?'

'So I have discovered in the last week or so that I am a stepping-stone to British nationality.'

Simnal groaned.

'Yes . . . once it was the case that if an Englishman married a foreign woman, the woman became a British national automatically on marriage . . . but the reverse didn't hold true. An Englishwoman marrying a foreigner took her husband's nationality. She could retain her own if she wished and have dual nationality, and that was the way of things until late in the twentieth century. After the passing of the anti-sex discrimination legislation, you see, a foreigner could apply for British citizenship after twenty-four months of marriage to an Englishwoman. Then, once they have the passport, they start divorce proceedings.'

'How do you know that is your husband's intention?'

She swilled the tea in her cup. 'Well . . . to use a word which you used . . . he was indiscreet. He has a friend, another doctor at the hospital where he works, Dr Kim from Thailand, and Dr Kim visited us. I heard my husband say, "Just another eight months and I'm a Brit Cit . . . just like you", and they both laughed. They didn't know I was outside the room. I felt as though I had been torn in half. I crept away and locked myself in the bathroom and wept until there were no more tears left.'

'I'm sorry.'

'Well, I'd rather know. I met the Kims once, they were an odd couple . . . he so small and finely built . . . she so large and round. Rebecca . . . she was called Rebecca . . . her parents didn't do their homework, Christian names have specific meanings.'

'I know.' Simnal smiled. 'Maurice means "of dark skin" for some reason.'

She smiled. 'Not appropriate in your case . . . fair skinned and blond hair, you are Nordic. Anyway, mine means "Beauty" or "Friend to all" depending on which reference you consult.'

'Well, yours is appropriate . . . the first meaning, anyway.'

'Thank you . . .' She blushed, quite appealingly, he thought.

'So what does Rebecca mean?'

'Born to adversity.'

'Oh . . . I'll avoid that name if ever I have a daughter.'

'Likewise, but in Rebecca Kim's case it seemed apt. Lovely personality but she had difficulty in attracting men . . . she was a nurse . . . then along came Dr Kim . . . showed interest and was a doctor . . . a woman's beauty and a man's status . . . they ought not to be important but they just are . . . and poor Becky struggled until Dr Kim came along and swept her off her feet. The marriage lasted two years. I don't know the quality of the marriage, we were not close, but after two years Dr Kim applied for citizenship, was awarded it, and then wasn't seen for dust . . . leaving Becky to pick up the pieces and sell the matrimonial home. They are both still working at the hospital. If they see each other, Dr Kim looks right through her . . . so I was told.' She shook her head. 'That's ahead of me. That's what my dearly beloved has in mind. I couldn't give myself to him after I heard that, but he doesn't seem to mind . . . just counting off the days.'

'Are you going to leave him?'

'Yes . . . but the divorce won't come through within eight months . . .'

'Give official notice of separation, that will stop him using you in the manner you describe.'

'Will it?' She looked at him earnestly.

'I'm certain, but I am not a lawyer. First thing Monday morning, straight to the solicitors.'

'Yes.' she smiled. 'Yes, I will.' She slid her hand across the table and held his and squeezed it. 'Maurice . . . Maurice . . . I don't want to go home. Not just yet . . . not ever at all really.'

Simnal too smiled. 'Ever visited Hutton Cranswick?'

'No . . .' she held eye contact with distended pupils, 'never. I've missed out there.'

'Time to rectify that omission in your life experience, I think.'

Four

'Nobody has made love to me like that for a long time.' Ruth turned and smiled at him. 'A very long time.'

Simnal and Ruth had left Selby and with Ruth at the wheel, had driven slowly back to Hutton Cranswick and to Simnal's house which stood on the edge of the village green. She parked outside the house and had looked over its edifice and expressed her being impressed.

'Yes, I like it.' Simnal had smiled his acknowledgement. 'Early Victorian . . . 1840 by the date above the door, but we don't know when the building was commenced, and interestingly, it has a stone cellar. Brick top hamper, from the ground up, but stone foundations.'

'It's on the site of an earlier building.'

'Yes, that's what we think . . . that's what I think now. Have to get used to "me think" rather than "we think".'

They had walked side by side up the drive, quite close again, touching hands and Simnal unlocked the front door and stepped back to allow Ruth to enter the house. He followed her, just catching the twitching of his neighbour's curtain as he did so. Inside the house, Ruth seemed as impressed as she was on the outside. Simnal watched as her eyes beheld the sweep of her first impressions . . . the wealth of panelling, the wide stairway. 'Very nice,' she had said. 'And so tidy.'

'Yes . . . it's hard work but I confess I enjoy it.' He later led her through to the kitchen. 'Tea, coffee?'

'You enjoy housework? You're a man in a million.'

'Well, it's fairly new to me it, it has that novelty about it . . . it takes my mind off things and I like the feeling of being on top of the house that I get when I have vacuumed and polished but the endlessness of it is beginning to get to me. I can well see myself taking a housekeep . . .' His voice trailed off as he turned to see that Ruth had not just taken off her summer jacket but her blouse as well, revealing pert and firm breasts which had little need of a bra.

'Let's stop playing games,' she had said.

It was later, lying side by side in Simnal's king-sized bed in the master bedroom that she had turned to him and said, 'No one has made love to me like that for a long time.'

For Maurice Simnal too, there was a feeling of 'not for a long time' about the experience. He was in his late thirties, a senior man in a senior profession. His life had slowed, had developed more depth, more nuances. Not since he was at university with long hair and faded denims had he stumbled and collapsed into bed with a girl so soon after their first meeting. For while he had known of Ruth for some weeks, it was not until the meal at the café in Selby some hours earlier had he felt they had become 'an item'.

'Reminds me of when I was younger,' he replied. She didn't ask for an explanation and he didn't offer one.

'So where do we go from here?' She turned her head away and looked at the ornate plaster ceiling, then glanced out of the window at the clear blue sky through which the sunlight was streaming. 'Don't think I have ever made love with open curtains before.'

'Can't be overlooked,' he said, stretching his arms. 'I never close them. Ever. West facing as you see . . . gets the sun in the afternoon and evening . . . and where from here? Well, it goes where we both want it to go . . . let's let "it" take us.'

'Yes.' She took his hand. 'I like that. Let's let it take us where it wants to take us. But we have to be discreet . . .

my husband is a jealous man . . . for him it's a one-way
street. He wants me for the passport. He isn't particularly
faithful . . . yet I am expected to be his and his alone.'

'Well . . . it's up to you . . . I won't get involved, but
you should leave him before he divorces you . . . if you're
sure of his intent about the passport.'

'I am sure.' She turned on her side and laid her arm
across his chest.

'Well it's early days yet, but there's space here, as you
see, if you need a place of shelter.'

She kissed his ribcage. 'Thank you. Where's your bathroom?'

'Down the corridor. Choice of two.'

'We don't need that . . .'

'What?'

'One each. Come on . . . I'm not a big girl and you are
not an oversized man . . . we can squeeze into the same
tub.'

Later he dressed in a full change of clothing, and she in
one of his spare clean shirts. He showed her the house, the
bedrooms, the study, the upstairs sitting room, the dining
room, the drawing room with settees and chairs lining the
wall, the expanse of Axminster carpet and the tabletop on
the floor – 'It was an old kitchen table . . . I chopped the
legs off it because I thought the floor area needed breaking
up.' He showed her the small television room – 'I just
won't have a television in the drawing room, it's like an
overbearing guest at a party.' He showed her Toby's room.
It was, she found, a typical small boy's room, with Thomas
the Tank Engine wallpaper and furry toys kept from an
earlier phase of life, and with books and toys of a stimu-
lating nature, age-appropriate for a seven-year-old, and
still, she thought, blessedly free of bigger boys' toys like
model soldiers and fighter planes, though she noted a
computer on a table by the window. It was, she thought, a
sign of the times, having mixed feelings about the microchip,

seeing its usefulness but disliking the way the world was growing dependent upon it.

'When do you see Toby again?' she asked as they left the room and walked back into the polish-scented upstairs corridor.

'Next weekend.'

'I'd like to meet him . . . would that be possible?'

'Yes.' Simnal smiled and nodded. 'Yes . . . I think I'd like him to meet you.'

They ate a meal, a summer snack, what Simnal described as a 'cold supper', pork pie, cheese, grapes, cold cooked meats, after which Ruth offered her apologies that she felt she must take her leave, explaining that she ought to be home before her husband returned from the golf club.

'Of course,' he said warmly. 'It's been very good.'

'When shall we see each other again?' She peeled off his shirt and stood, naked, by the kitchen table. 'Where shall I put this?'

'Over the chair . . . I'll see to it. See each other again? Whenever you like . . . whenever you can. You are the one who is more constrained by circumstances' than me.'

'Tomorrow?' She dropped the shirt over the chair. 'How about tomorrow?'

'Suits me . . . sooner than I expected . . . but it suits me.'

'Well, his esteemed self, God bless him, is going sailing tomorrow . . . he is the co-owner of a small yacht. He'll be away early . . . Humber yachtsmen have to be wary of the tide . . . the ebb will take him out and they'll potter about off the coast and catch the flood about six p.m. . . . he'll be home by nine p.m. So long as I leave here no later than eight . . .'

'Sounds exquisite,' he said. 'Sounds perfect.'

'Good.' She leaned forward and kissed his forehead. 'I'll be here about ten. Earlier if I can manage.'

In the event she arrived at ten-fifteen, panting her

apologies. One hour later, and once again lying side by side in Simnal's bed with the curtains open, revealing a vast blue sky, she told him that she had 'really missed' him, that just the one night away from him had been 'minute by minute torture'.

'It was difficult for me too,' he said. 'I just seemed to get fed up with my own company and I strolled across the green for a pint or two . . . it killed the evening . . . brought sleep earlier, brought the morning sooner . . . seemed to, anyway.'

After a pause she said, 'Hungry?'

'Ravenous.'

'I've brought some food . . . made lunch for us . . . another reason why I was a bit late . . . chicken salad sound good?'

'Perfect . . . just right for a day like today.'

After lunch they drove into York and were tourists for the afternoon. They walked the walls with other tourists, pottered and poked around gift shops, went up the Minster tower and gazed down upon the medieval houses and narrow streets beneath, they explored the snickelways, the enchanting system of narrow passageways that is like a street system within the street system. They watched a juggler adept with three coloured balls and were happy to drop a few coins into his hat, as they were happy to drop coins into the hat in front of a clearly skilled female violinist who filled the crowd-thronged streets with uplifting music. In the early evening they joined the 'ghost walk', guided by an actor in Victorian dress touring the city's ghost sighting locations and listening to the story attached to each. Particularly enthralling, they both agreed, was the story of a column of Roman soldiers who seemed to appear out of the wall, marching, it seemed, past a tradesman who was working close by and frightening him out of his wits in the process. They also admitted to being 'a bit pleased' that the most often seen ghost in England, with an average of two sightings a year, didn't show herself. It would, they thought, have been too distressing. The story went that she was abandoned by her parents when she showed symptoms of the plague, who left the house, having painted a large yellow cross on the door, thus condemning their daughter to certain death. If the plague didn't kill her, thirst and starvation would have done. Her ghost is to be seen standing at the window, as if looking for her parents returning.

They dined at an Italian restaurant and then drove back to Hutton Cranswick, where they agreed they had time for just a coffee before Ruth had to leave in order to be home to welcome 'the weary mariner'.

'I'll phone you,' she said as she sat in her car and started the engine.

'Please do . . . any time.' He put a finger to his lips then put it to hers. 'I won't phone you.'

'You can phone my work number . . . but not my home number.'

'We must see each other soon.'

'Very soon.'

'We can decide now, can't we? How about Wednesday afternoon?'

'Yes . . . we are both psychologists . . . we structure our own day. I don't know what I am doing on Wednesday but I know I haven't got a conference or a meeting to attend. I can rearrange my appointments.'

'Well, I am just working on my research project and anything that the Humphrey Sweet case throws up. I can take the afternoon off.'

'That's a date.' She smiled and nodded. 'I'll phone you tomorrow on your mobile . . . firm things up then . . . once I've had a look at my diary. Thanks . . . thanks, Maurice. It's been a good day . . . a really good day.'

'It's a flower,' Tom Mautby said. 'Or flowers . . . so far as we can tell. If you see anything else, please tell us.' He handed the photographs of the murder of Edward Stamner and of the three schoolgirls to Simnal.

'Flowers?' Simnal reached forward and picked up the photographs, both black and white and colour. 'That's interesting. The charge nurse at the hospital, he reported Sweet had started making references to flowers and singing that song . . . what is it? "Flowers of the Forest".'

'Really?' Mautby breathed in. 'Now, that is interesting.'

'Isn't it? So what do we have?'

'Well, flowers it seems . . . not in the crime scene as such but just outside, caught by chance by the camera . . . in the foreground of the distant shots. Look.' Mautby pointed to the bottom corner of the photographs of Edward Stamner's flat. 'You see a daffodil lying on the ground . . .'

'Yes.'

'It's actually outside the police tape. Nobody saw it as relevant at the time, if they noticed it at all . . . it's just a flower on the edge of a footpath next to the lawn . . . nothing particularly unusual.'

'Nothing at all,' Simnal conceded.

'It becomes relevant when we look at the crime scene photograph of two of the three schoolgirls. You remember he was found holding the body of the third girl?'

'Yes.'

'So no photographs were taken of him . . . but the earlier two crime scenes show a flower to be present on the edge.' Mautby collected the photographs of the scene of Edward Stamner's murder, and placed them back in the file. He then handed Simnal another set of photographs. 'Really, it's just the top one . . . the one that shows the crime scene from a distance. Again, the focus is the body in the woodland but again . . . in the foreground, a flower . . . on the ground just caught by the camera.'

'Yes . . . a rose . . . looks like . . . yellow anyway. I wonder if yellow has a significance for him?'

'Again, not seen as relevant at the time and it's just luck

it was caught on film, or as if he knew where the scene-of-crime officer would be standing.'

Simnal picked up the photograph. 'You know in hindsight . . . lovely, lovely hindsight . . . it is relevant, as is Sweet's recently developed habit of singing "Flowers of the Forest".'

'What does it mean?' Mautby smiled.

'Well . . . forest is in fact originally a legal term to denote land use.'

'Is it?'

'Yes. Now it's come to mean a large wood but after the conquest, William the Conqueror had large tracts of land set aside for hunting purposes . . . and these lands were governed by "Forest Law" which meant that game on the land could not be taken by the rank and file . . . it could only be hunted by William and members of his court.'

'I didn't know that.'

'It's true . . . and consequently a forest is composed of large tracts of open country as well as woodland.'

'Yes?' Mautby's eyebrows narrowed. Simnal saw that he was clearly curious as to where his history lesson was leading.

'Well . . . in large open areas you would expect wild flowers to grow . . . these would be flowers of the forest.'

'Yes . . .'

'But how often have you seen flowers in woodland?'

'Not often.' Mautby stroked his chin.

'Hardly ever . . . the floor of a wood doesn't contain many flowers.'

'I take your point . . . but my wife and I . . . when we were courting, as was the expression, or "going steady" . . . before we were married . . . one glorious hot summer's day made love on a bed of bluebells in a wood.'

Simnal smiled as he and Mautby held eye contact. 'A memory to savour.'

'Oh yes,' Mautby sighed. 'Tell me, professor, where did my youth go?'

'Same way as mine . . . but it's better than dying young. It has that compensation.'

'Oh yes . . . I think we all have contemporaries who are no longer with us.'

'Indeed, but my point is that a rose lying on the ground of a woodland is very out of place . . . a daffodil lying by the side of a path in an elderly people's accommodation is also . . . unusual. It looked a quite new . . . quite fresh flower. If someone was carrying a bunch of flowers and dropped one . . . they'd pick it up . . . you'd think so anyway.'

'Yes . . . or if a warm-hearted person saw a recently cut daffodil lying on the ground they'd pick it up and take it home and put it in a jar of water.'

'Yes.' Mautby again stroked his chin. 'I see where you are going . . . he's dropping flowers . . . that's his calling card . . . but not on the person . . . in the vicinity.'

'It would seem so.'

'We still need him to tell us which other people he has murdered. We can't sift through the photographs of the scenes of unsolved murders looking for a flower at the edges of the photographs . . . haven't the manpower . . . and he hunts far and wide . . . outside our area. An out-of-place flower in a photograph of the crime scene might confirm it's one of his . . . but since he's giving up his dead . . . it's redundant.'

'Yes . . . we were meant to see the significance of the flowers, but we didn't.'

'We couldn't be expected to see the significance at the time . . . different police forces investigating different types of murder wouldn't see the connection. If he wanted the significance of the flowers to be seen, he should have made them more obvious . . . so he's telling us now. He wants the credit, the recognition that is due to him . . . or rather he feels is due to him.'

'Credit . . . recognition . . . what makes these people tick?'

'That is what the Home Office is paying me to find out.' Simnal stood. 'They didn't know it would open an investigation.'

'When do you see him again?'

'Sweet? Friday . . . I visit every Friday. Ruth Day . . . she's the psychiatrist at Kempton . . . she sees him twice a week also. We put our heads together when I go over there. I still have my research project to address, so just once a week . . . at his pace. We're putting a little pressure on him now, but not so much that he'd "clam up" and it's not as though this inquiry has any urgency, like we said . . . the dead are dead and he's not in a position to take further victims.' Simnal put on his panama.

'Do you think he's mad or bad? Off the record.'

'Off the record, I'd say mad . . . he's showing signs of having Multiple Personality Disorder.'

'You mean there's more than one of him?' Mautby chuckled. 'That would be too much to cope with.'

That evening Tom Mautby took a bunch of flowers home to his wife. 'Talked to a trick cyclist today,' he explained, 'talked about flowers in woodland . . .'

Florence Mautby blushed.

'Just had to bring these home, they're not bluebells, but . . .'

Florence and Tom Mautby embraced and were both delighted to find that the passion and the magic had not at all disappeared from their relationship, rather it proved to be as strong as it was on that day in the wood. It also had developed a depth over the years, so Tom Mautby felt as he and his wife lay side by side as the sun set, and he pondered that growing old is not without its compensations.

*   *   *

On the Wednesday of that week, shortly after lunch, Maurice Simnal wrote, 'Out – back tomorrow a.m.', Blu-tacked it to his office door and left the Department of Health's offices on St Leonard's Place and drove home to Hutton Cranswick. He experienced mixed feelings as he drove. There was the elation, the thrill of the anticipated sexual encounter with Ruth; there was the sense that his life was becoming whole once more. There was also a sense that he was betraying Jane again . . . what was the term the police used when felons dig themselves in deeper? . . . Compounding the felony . . . that's it . . . he felt he was compounding the felony, but Jane was an unforgiving woman; was he actually compounding the felony or was he exercising his freedom of choice as a separated man? He had walked across the green to the pub the last two evenings and stood at the bar, not wanting to be part of the conversation, yet not wanting to be home alone either. Ruth was interesting, she was intelligent, she was attractive, and being trapped in a poisonous marriage gave her an added appeal of vulnerability. Yet she just wasn't Jane, and his self-recrimination at losing Jane ate deep within him, like a termite inside a length of timber. He slowed as he approached his home and smiled, and his heart thumped as he saw her sitting in her car outside his house. The remainder of the afternoon he thought pleasant, exciting, thrilling, but somehow . . . somehow also disappointing. Ruth was not Jane . . . he could not rid himself of the feeling that she was an intruder, an interloper. When they parted there was a mutual reluctance, but he felt the reluctance was greater on her part than it was on his.

When they met again the following Friday there was a warmth between them, with the occasional knowing eye contact, but the conversation was strictly business.

'I saw him twice this week,' Ruth consulted her notes, 'he's talking . . . still singing "Flowers of the Forest" whenever myself or the nurses are within earshot. He's telling us something there, I know he is . . . can't think what it might be . . . the nurses haven't a clue either.'

'He is telling us something.' Simnal raised his eyebrows, and told her.

'Well, well . . .' Ruth sat back in her chair. 'Well, well . . . so his hallmark was too obscure to be noticed . . . and you are right, there are not many flowers in a wood. With the advantage of hindsight perhaps the rose on the floor of the wood should have been seen as being out of place.'

'If it was near the body, I'm sure that it would have been,' Simnal cleared his throat, 'but that's the other thing about the flowers, he dropped them sufficiently far from the body that they were not seen as part of the crime scene. The police have to draw a boundary somewhere.'

'I suppose they must.'

'Anyway, the police didn't see his hallmark so now he's telling us . . . wants the recognition.' Simnal stood. 'Well, I'll cut along and see him. I'll tell him about the flowers. I'm sure he'll be very pleased.'

'I am very pleased.' Humphrey Sweet looked at Simnal with his large, warm, approving eyes. Eyes that could so easily influence a child or a teenager, even a gullible adult, but which sent a shiver down Simnal's spine. 'I thought the police were slow. So I decided to tell you.'

'We are grateful.'

'Who saw the pattern? You?'

Simnal shook his head. 'No, it was a police officer.'

'Name?'

'Can't tell you . . . but you pointed us in the right direction with your new-found fondness for that song.'

'The Flowers of the Forest?'

'Yes . . . it was the police officer who pointed out that there really are very few flowers in woodland . . . so the rose lying some distance from the schoolgirl's body then became significant, as did the daffodil outside the elderly gentleman's flat.'

'Ah yes . . . the old boy . . . he put up a struggle.'

'But the flowers were not noticed by the police because you left them too far from the body and they didn't sit up and sing.'

'Sit up and sing . . .' Sweet smiled. 'I like your use of the language. Something more obvious and the pattern would have been seen . . . or if I had left the flowers on the body . . . yes, that was a mistake. We'll learn from that.'

'We?'

'Lenny and Alf and me.'

Simnal nodded. 'I would like to meet them . . . may I meet them?'

'Not today. They are not ready to meet you. Perhaps in a while.'

'All right. But it would be interesting to meet them.'

'Whenever.' Sweet continued to hold eye contact with Simnal. 'And you and the lovely Dr Day visited my little parents and little Selby . . . that was good of you. Though perhaps you were not concerned for their welfare.'

'We were trying to obtain background information about you.'

'I thought as much.'

'So what did you do to the rabbit and the goldfish?' Simnal pursed his lips. 'And the cat, your kitten Pitch?'

'Pitch . . . I tied a brick to its collar . . . you know the type, an air brick . . . a brick with holes in it.'

'Yes.'

'Took it down to the river . . . just near where we lived.'

'And threw it in?'

'No,' Sweet sneered. 'I've never killed quickly . . . never . . . I believe people and animals should know that they are going to die . . . kinder . . . it allows them to prepare. So I took Pitch down to the river where it was quite quiet . . . and left her by the water's edge . . . fun . . .'

'Fun?'

'Yes . . . a gamble. Would she be rescued before the water level rises and sweeps her away to meet her maker? Didn't hear of anyone rescuing her so I reckon the water must have got her . . . or another animal . . . a fox . . . a rat . . . Would a rat attack a kitten?'

'I really don't know.'

'I suppose if the rat was big enough . . . if the kitten was exhausted and weak enough. Anyway, who cares? We'll never know.' He paused. 'The rabbit . . . the rabbit I strangled. He put up a struggle just like the old man . . . kept releasing the pressure, then reapplying it . . . that's when I first saw fear in the other person's eyes . . . even though it was a rabbit, just a rabbit . . . that thing knew fear when it was dying. The eyes bulge you know.'

'Yes,' Simnal said quietly, 'yes, I do know that.'

'Why, have you done it . . . are you really one of us?' Sweet's face seemed to brighten up.

'No.' Simnal spoke firmly. 'Let's just say I know what fear looks like in a person's eyes. Professionally.'

'Oh,' Sweet looked disappointed, so thought Simnal, 'I thought for a moment . . .'

'Well, you're wrong.'

'Anyway. The rabbit . . . came a time I didn't take the pressure off its throat. It was scratching away like mad . . . but I didn't take the pressure off.' Sweet spoke, it seemed to Simnal with a profound sense of pride. 'Then I tossed the thing into the river. The goldfish . . . well, the old goldfish . . . that went down the toilet . . . after I starved it to death.'

'You starved it?'

'Yes . . . I put it in the water tank behind the toilet . . . the flush tank . . . then put the lid back on . . . it's a low flush in our house. Checked on it three days later . . . floating there . . . no food and total darkness for three days . . . then I fished it out and flushed it down the tubes.'

Simnal paused. He then asked Sweet what he felt like when he was torturing and killing his pets.

'Powerful.' The reply was instantaneous. 'I really felt very powerful. Especially with the rabbit . . . letting it think it might live, then squeezing its throat again.'

Simnal allowed a brief moment of silence, then he said, 'You said the old boy, Mr Stamner, put up a struggle . . .'

'They all did,' Sweet smiled. 'All of them.'

'All? Including the schoolgirls?'

'Especially the schoolgirls . . . they didn't want to die. Never gave up . . . even when I told them it was hopeless.'

'You, or we?'

'Just me with the schoolgirls . . . Alf and Lenny . . . they just were not there.'

'How is your status on the ward?'

'Increasing . . . I am enjoying some good publicity and it'll go on increasing.'

'Seems to be the case . . . the more you tell me . . . the more we tell the press . . . the more media coverage . . . and hey . . . you're the man.'

'That's how it works,' Sweet smirked. 'The others in here' – he half turned and looked over his shoulder with a sneer of contempt – 'the others don't have any skeletons in their closets . . . don't seem to have, anyway, because we've all got some . . . haven't we, Maurice? Bet you've got a few.'

'We are not here to talk about me, Humphrey.'

'They must have . . . all criminally insane in here and the nature of committing crime is that you get away with so much, or so many, and then get captured for one . . . then the boys in blue try to stick other crimes on your track . . . if they can, helps make their arrest rates look good. So either these in here coughed to everything for a reduced sentence . . . or they kept mum, like me.'

'Until now. You kept mum, until now.'

'That's because I'm getting better . . . the hospital is

curing me.' Again he smiled. 'You and Ruth are very good at your jobs. How are you getting on by the way? Pleasant lady, isn't she . . . very pleasant. Pity I'll never know just how pleasant . . . but you might tell me. Would you tell me?'

'You know better than that, Humphrey.' Simnal looked down at his notes, avoiding eye contact. He thought Sweet more confident, more forward than usual; he was, as the Irish would say, more 'bold' than hitherto. He then looked up and deliberately held eye contact with Sweet, looking, staring at him. It was a tried and tested technique for making people not just talk, but cut to the chase. On this occasion it worked, Simnal thought, wonderfully.

'Six years ago,' Sweet said, 'I think . . . the dates will be easy to find, but it was five or six years ago in Bristol. Strange place, Bristol . . . do you know it?'

'No. I've been there only once or twice . . . so, no, I don't know it at all. The Wills monument, the suspension bridge . . . the railway station called "Temple Meads" . . . some English railway stations have such poetic names . . .'

'Don't they . . . Carlisle Citadel, Edinburgh Waverley . . . that's in Scotland, but it's still poetic . . . Hull Paragon . . .'

'Not any more . . . they cut the name down.'

'Preston Measles . . . hardly poetic, but pretty weird giving a railway station a name which is also the name of an illness . . . it's like York Chickenpox or something.' Sweet sniggered at his own joke, then his eyebrows suddenly narrowed. 'Didn't know about Hull . . . pity that. What is it now? Just plain old Hull?'

'Last time I visited, yes.'

'Don't like that. Hull Paragon was a lovely name.'

Simnal thought Sweet looked indignant, as though, Simnal further thought, that Sweet had taken the name change of the railway station as a personal affront, as though he resented having not been consulted about the matter.

'Anyway . . . what happened in Bristol?'

The smile of self-satisfaction returned to Sweet's face. His eyes seemed to light up. 'Stabbed a boy,' he said. 'It was the messiest I've done. Had a car. Wouldn't have got away with it otherwise . . . full tank of petrol. Night-time . . . about two a.m., or three . . . summer time but still dark. I drove there from Selby . . . my own car . . . didn't borrow one from the dealership. I could do that . . . borrow cars from the dealership . . . but I had a notion it might be messy so I took my car, didn't want to bloody up the dealership car . . . too many questions would be asked. So, drove down . . . left Selby at . . . well, late afternoon was in Bristol, parked up a side street . . . real big houses, I was parked up by ten p.m., just sitting in the car. Few people went by, but I was waiting until it was quiet . . . waiting for a person by themselves. This was going to be a stabbing . . . wouldn't be linked to anything else I'd done . . . or might be doing in the future and well away from Selby. I mean, who'd suspect little me?'

'Who indeed? Tell me about it.' Simnal spoke softly, invitingly. 'Why don't you start at the beginning?'

'Difficult to know when that was.'

'Well . . . when the notion to take another life took hold.'

'Can't recall really. The notion, as you call it, grows in my head, sort of swirls around . . . getting bigger until it becomes something I can't ignore . . . it takes over.'

'Yes.'

'Probably a week . . . possibly the Monday of the week. I drove to Bristol on the Friday . . . so four, five days . . . that sort of time period.'

'I see.' Simnal paused. 'Grew in your head?'

'Yes. That's what I said and that's what it's like.'

'Did Alf and Lenny take part in the planning?'

'Not for the Bristol job.'

'So they weren't there?'

'No.'

'What about on the way down or back?'

'No. Just me for the young guy in Bristol . . . just me throughout.'

Simnal wrote on his pad. 'So why Bristol?'

'It's easy to get to . . . a long way from the Vale of York. Tell you the truth, I didn't plan to go to Bristol . . . didn't even plan to go south . . . I started driving with murder in mind. Reckon there's some young fella in Newcastle right now who's alive because I decided to go south, not north . . . it's fate . . . can't avoid it.'

'There's a lot of ill luck involved sometimes . . . just being in the wrong place at the wrong time . . . whether that amounts to fate . . . that's not for me to say.'

'Oh, it is,' Sweet smiled. 'It's fate all right. That's one of the reasons I allowed myself to be caught. I was controlling the destiny of too many people . . . I was controlling people's fate . . . that isn't comfortable. I like the power . . . but not that much power. I got frightened after a while.'

'And you wanted the recognition. Not a great deal of point in murdering so many people unless you get the recognition.'

'Some do.'

'You think?'

'Oh, yes . . . the maddies in here all knew each other on the outside.'

'Really?'

'Yes, really . . . they meet . . . birds of a feather . . . like finds like . . . like criminals get to know each other. The mad ones are the same . . . meet in the outpatients . . . have had periods of hospitalization . . . they meet there, meet up in the same pub . . . they form a network . . . a very useful network, because they are the only people they can boast of their crimes to. So you hear people talk about knowing someone . . . who knows someone . . . who did the murder . . . did the arson attack . . . got away with a hit and run . . . and believe me, Dr Simnal . . .'

'Thank you. I am happier with formal address.'

'Dr Simnal . . . I'll remember that.'

'If you would.'

'Anyway, you can take it from me, there are more serial killers out there than you realize . . . and they aren't recognized because they are doing what I did, different MOs, different victim profile, different area of the country for each murder. That way the murders are not linked, that way they keep one step ahead of the police. Me . . . I decided to blow the whistle. Since you and the lovely Dr Day have taken an interest in my case, I want the recognition for what I did . . . but I want to blow the whistle . . . I want it to be called the "Sweet Syndrome". Can you do that for me, Dr Simnal? The second level of serial killing . . . different types of victim, different MOs, travelling the length and breadth of the country, named after the first serial killer of this type to be identified, Humphrey Sweet.' Sweet sat back in his chair and seemed to Simnal to be enjoying great satisfaction and contentment.

'I might.' Simnal thought it indeed a possibility. His paper on 'variable serial killers' was already forming in his mind. Identifying a newly discovered syndrome would propel him to the forefront of the field of forensic psychology and each syndrome had to have a name, and why not 'the Sweet Syndrome'? Quite fair and reasonable to name it after the first such variable killer to be identified. 'It's a possibility. You help me. I'll help you.'

'The Sweet Syndrome.' Humphrey Sweet smiled and glanced up at the ceiling. 'I like it . . . it has a ring to it. My name gives it a double meaning . . . yes . . . it will mark my passage through life. Yes, I like it.'

'Well it starts here, Humphrey.'

'Starts?' Sweet gave Simnal a cold look. 'It's already started . . . I thought I've been co-operating.'

'You have. All right . . . sorry . . . it continues here. Yes . . . continue with this level of co-operation and I'll propose the name . . . no reason why it shouldn't be adopted. No reason at all. So, Bristol?'

'Toyed with him. Scared the life out of him. Yes I did. I was bigger than him . . . he was a small boy, late teens . . . by small, I mean really weedy . . . hunched forward as he shuffled along the pavement . . . again, fate. It was getting time to return, I was about to give up, then this figure comes up on the other side of the street . . . ideal . . . alone . . . small . . . male. I thought I was going to lose him but would you believe it? He begins to cross the road. Then I knew it was the right thing to do . . . it was right to kill him because if it wasn't, fate wouldn't have made him cross the road, would it?'

'So then what?'

'I let him walk past, got out, put a knife to his throat, backed him up into a bit of waste ground between two houses. Not a rubbish tip . . . the area was too posh for that . . . really big houses.'

'Yes.'

'Made him strip off . . . all his clothes . . . he was quivering with fear . . . the fear in his eyes . . . puny little guy, whimpering voice . . . oh but the power, Dr Simnal, the power. Left a flower in the gutter. A tulip, I think.'

Simnal remained silent but kept his eyes fixed on Humphrey Sweet.

'Well, then I knifed him . . . it was getting cold . . . we hadn't been disturbed at all . . . I didn't want to push my luck . . . shoved the blade into him, nice and easy . . . found his heart . . . felt the tremor in the blade . . . felt his life give out. Then I drove back to Selby. I was home for lunchtime.'

Outside the ward Simnal paused. He stood in the heat

of the late afternoon sun, a windless day, hardly any cloud, a long white vapour trail of a jet airliner streaked across the high blue dome yet all he could feel was a deep chill.

Five

Maurice and Jane Simnal met at ten p.m. at Lendal Bridge. She held Toby's hand as they appeared. Toby's face lit up like a sunburst upon recognizing his father and he tugged at his mother's hand. Unlike Toby, Jane kept her head down, avoiding eye contact until the last moment. The exchange was formal and dignified.

'Hello,' he said.

'Hello,' she replied, as Toby, freed from his mother's hand, grabbed his father's leg.

'Anything I should know?' Simnal cupped his hands around Toby's head, ruffling the mop of blond hair.

'No.' She handed Simnal a blue bag containing Toby's change of clothes and toiletries for the weekend. 'Nothing. Same as it was two weeks ago.'

'I see. How are you?'

She glanced at him. The question was evidently unexpected, a touch of tenderness amid the acrimony. 'I'm OK. And you?'

Maurice Simnal smiled. 'I am well, thank you.'

'Good.' She smiled and nodded. 'Good.'

'You don't plan a holiday this year?'

'No money.' She moved against the bridge parapet as a throng of people, all tourists, walked past. 'What about you?'

'Well . . . money's tight . . . but if there's no one to go on holiday with . . . well, then I'd prefer to stay at home.'

'Yes, I know what you mean.' She paused. 'So you haven't found anyone?'

97

'I might have.' He saw her head slump. The news clearly distressed her. He felt her pain. 'Have you?'

'I haven't been looking.' She forced a smile. 'The Starship Trooper here is a full-time job, as you may remember.'

'Yes.' He felt a sense of loss.

'Yes.' She knelt, kissed Toby and urged him to be a good boy and then turned on her heels, blonde hair and blue blouse rapidly consumed in a crowd of foot passengers all equally lightly dressed. Maurice Simnal sensed that she had forced herself to turn and walk away, and he was surprised at the strength of his wish that she would remain.

Jane Simnal returned home with a heavy heart and sank into an armchair, and, using the remote, switched on the television, her only company when Toby was with his father. She didn't notice the screen, didn't pay attention to the dialogue . . . her anger towards him had, she had found, turned slowly but certainly into an anger towards herself. 'What,' she thought, 'what, what, what have I done?' . . . She pondered: she had been married to an interesting, successful man. She had run at him with a kitchen knife . . . she had spitefully, so very spitefully smashed up his late father's collection of Royal Doulton . . . that . . . that had been just so, so . . . spiteful of her. It was only when he had gone . . . only when she was alone in bed at night, with nobody beside her to slide his arms around her, only then did she realize how much she had loved him, and still did love him. It was, she thought with a pain in her chest and stomach, a pain caused by emotion and nothing else, it was so, so true . . . it is only when it is gone that one truly realizes what one had.

Maurice and Toby walked through the summer streets of York, the musicians, of varying degrees of competency, the man on stilts, the jugglers, all performing for passing coins, the beggars with puppies on a string . . . the horse-drawn carriage, the open-topped buses, the high blue sky and the relentless sun that caused the pavements to bake. Together they picked their way through the snickelways, finding new ones to explore, each narrow alley holding a special delight for Toby. They had lunch in a restaurant opposite the Minster. When they had finished eating, Maurice Simnal said, 'There's somebody I want you to meet . . . I want you to be a good boy . . . best behaviour, understood?'

Toby nodded.

'She's a lady. Just a friend of mine. We thought we'd go to the railway museum . . . would you like that?'

'Please . . .' Toby's face lit up . . .

'Her name's Ruth . . .' Simnal glanced up. 'In fact, here she is.' He stood, smiled . . . he and Ruth kissed gently . . . a kiss of greeting, not of passion.

During the drive home to Hutton Cranswick, Simnal felt complete again: he at the wheel, a lady beside him, his son in the rear seat. All very picture-perfect, but it was also somehow incomplete . . . the passion he felt for Ruth was not the passion, not the depth, not the richness that he had felt, and part of him still did feel, for Jane . . . and the little boy on the rear seat was not their creation. An observer would see them drive by and think 'family', but Simnal knew it was not a family, only half of one, with a friend. Toby seemed to have taken to Ruth from the outset and Ruth, he saw, had been perfect with Toby . . . not overeager to be friendly, not pushing herself on him, but responding warmly when he spoke to her, allowing and encouraging him to grow towards her.

That evening they ate a wholesome meal prepared with care and skill by Ruth. Later she played Scrabble with Toby while Simnal washed the dishes.

'Happy families,' she said, sitting on the settee, after Toby had gone to bed and was settled if not fully asleep.

'Indeed.' Simnal returned the smile. 'This afternoon was good. Very good. Thank you.'

'I enjoyed it. Toby's a lovely little boy.'

'Yes . . . I saw you two seemed to take a shine to each other. He relaxed very quickly in your presence. He doesn't often do that. I expected him to be quite shy . . . in fact, very shy at first . . . but . . . well done, you. It's a pity you have to return . . .'

'Yes . . . I'd like to stay, but Abdul . . . he's unpredictable . . . he intended to take the *Free Radical* up the coast to Scarborough or even Whitby if the wind was fair, but I know him . . . he might decide to return on an impulse. I can't take the chance of not being at home this evening. When do you return Toby?'

'Five p.m. at Lendal Bridge. Jane wants another meeting place . . . I said I'd find one somewhere not so crowded.'

'That won't be easy this time of year . . .'

'Oh, it will.' Simnal sipped his sherry. 'There are plenty of little nooks and crannies in York. There's a small, ancient graveyard just behind Micklegate . . . I swear you could cavort naked in the middle of the day there and not be seen, yet you'd be in the centre of the city. It's that sort of place. Intriguing. Toby and I are exploring the snickelways . . . we did a few before you joined us.'

'Sounds fun.'

'Well, we'll do the same tomorrow if you'd care to join us?'

'I'd love to. If Abdul keeps the boat overnight he'll be home late tomorrow. He's single-handing so he doesn't have any crew members' wishes to take into consideration.'

Later Simnal walked Ruth to the front gate. It was a calm, warm, still evening, still light at eight-thirty. High above, swallows and swifts dived and twisted in the hunt for flying insects, which had been pushed high above the ground by the day's thermal currents; vapour trails criss-crossed a crimson sky.

'It's going to be a pleasant day tomorrow,' she said.

'More pleasant if you can join us.' He kissed her.

'I'll phone you in the morning. I'll know whether yea or nay then. He'll either be there or he won't. So I'll be able to join you or I won't.'

'Simple as that. Sorry I can't walk you to the railway station,' he pointed over his shoulder, 'but I can't leave the Starship Trooper unattended. Wouldn't want to.'

'The Starship Trooper,' she said with a laugh.

'That's what Jane has started calling him. It seems to fit somehow. He has a chunkiness about him. Moves like a man already and he's seven years old.'

'Well, until tomorrow. If I can . . .'

'Yes. Until tomorrow. If you can.'

Ruth was able to join Maurice and Toby Simnal the following day and all three enjoyed a pleasant day in the Simnal house. It was a typical Sunday of a non-religious family, a cooked breakfast despite the heat, after which Ruth and Simnal disappeared behind newspapers which, once read, were discarded on the floor whilst Toby amused himself with his computer. Later, at Simnal's insistence that they were 'not going to waste a day like today', the three strolled across the vast green on Hutton Cranswick, fed the ducks on the pond, at which point Simnal took the opportunity to draw Ruth's attention to the nearby war memorial and the name of the Home Guardsman inscribed thereon.

'The only war memorial I know of with the name of a Home Guardsman on it,' he said, shielding his eyes from the sun's glare as he read it.

'Do you know the story?' She linked her arm with his.

'I don't. It's often intrigued me. I'll ask at the pub some time. There's a good few old people in the village.'

They walked on, down Main Street, in sunhats and short sleeves, across the railway line and into the field system, took the first road on the left, and walked through a flat and richly cultivated landscape beneath an arching blue sky. At the crossroads they turned left and followed the road back into Hutton Cranswick, and kept bearing left until they came to the green again, and thence home. A pleasant hour's stroll, taking the day, taking the air, letting the breakfast settle and managing to prise Toby away from the computer screen for a brief period of exercise and stimulation. Back at the house, Ruth went to the kitchen and, wrapping herself in a blue apron, began to prepare the roast leg of lamb. She cooked alone, at her insistence, and at four p.m. they sat down to enjoy what Simnal thought to be an excellent meal.

'Just time to get Toby back to Lendal Bridge.' Simnal folded his napkin. 'But thanks . . . that was excellent.'

'I'll have to leave too,' she said. 'The sailor will be home from the sea . . .'

'Of course.'

'I'll phone you.'

'Yes,' he smiled, 'please do.'

'His name was Mark Frost.' Tom Mautby read from his notes. 'The Avon and Somerset police asked me to convey their appreciation.'

Simnal opened a palm in response. 'I am pleased to have been of service.' He sipped his tea.

'They want to come up and interview Sweet.'

'Understandable.'

'They're happy to wait though . . . I explained what we are finding out . . . they don't want to upset the apple cart so they'll take a back seat for a while. They have other unsolved murders . . .'

'I think they'll remain unsolved. I doubt if Sweet was involved, especially if they show similarities. He murders once in one area, different type of victim, different MO. If any other young males were stabbed in the Bristol area at the time, then . . . well, it, or they, won't be down to Humphrey Sweet.'

'You're getting to know him.'

'Quite well.' Simnal leaned forward and placed the empty mug on Mautby's desk. 'I am so pleased he is where he is. He's the most frightening man I have ever met. He seems to have given up trying to manipulate and control me, which is something of a relief, it was tiring to resist it all the time . . . a challenge of two minds.'

'Which you won.' Mautby smiled a warm, approving smile.

'It's not quite the same as winning. I wasn't victorious, he wasn't defeated. It's more of the case that my castle walls were strong enough to withstand his attack. If he had carried on I might have given in eventually on the basis that every siege succeeds if it can be sustained long enough. But he clearly felt the effort wasn't worth the gain. There are others he can control much more easily. One of whom apparently is a certain Kathleen Hood.'

'Who's she?'

'A frequent correspondent and visitor.'

'Interesting.'

'Yes, I have come across such before . . . not at all uncommon . . . easily led people who have a fascination with individuals like Humphrey Sweet. Such folk merit a study in their own right, if you ask me.'

'You'll be visiting her?'

'This week. I'll ask Ruth Day to accompany me. We're co-working "the Sweet case", as it's become known. It's taking more and more of my time, but I am still here to complete a course of research into people like Humphrey Sweet, I must not lose sight of that.'

'Appreciated that, but your help here has been invaluable, a case we never knew existed is cracking wide open . . . it really is astounding. What are you going to call him, "variable serial killer?"'

'Yes . . . I think so. A recently identified phenomenon just makes you wonder how many more of his ilk are out there.'

'Yes.' Mautby sat back in his chair – heavy-boned, serious facial expression. His office window overlooked the Ouse on which pleasure craft carried summer tourists. 'That thought had occurred to me. If a killer can strangle, he can also use a knife. If he kills a woman, he can also kill a man. If he kills indoors, he can just as easily kill out of doors . . . and we would never link the crimes.'

'Until now.' Simnal raised his eyebrows.

'Aye . . . and complicated by the fact that he kills in areas covered by different police forces who, well, who could be better at talking to each other.'

'In fairness, there's no reason why the Lancashire police would think you might be interested in an old lady who was bludgeoned to death in their patch, when they hear about a young student who was knifed to death in your patch.'

'Aye . . .'

'So what did the Somerset and Avon boys tell you about Mark Frost?'

'He was knifed . . . multiple stab wounds . . . body was naked, but they ruled out a sexually motivated crime.'

'Yes . . . Sweet was on a power trip. He told me he made the boy strip before he killed him. It will be in my report.'

'Really?'

'Yes, really.'

'They're sending some crime scene photographs up for our reference. They don't show a flower anywhere . . . apparently, not one that was laid at the scene anyway. Possibly some wild ones growing on the waste ground but not a hallmark.'

'He said it was possibly a tulip. Laid in the gutter.'

Mautby shrugged. 'No reason for them to link it to the crime.'

'None.'

'So what now for you?'

'A trip to see one Miss Hood.'

'Ah, yes . . . the correspondent and visitor. Should be interesting.'

'I'll let you know what happens.' Simnal stood. 'Well, I'd better get back to St Leonard's . . . paperwork to catch up on, the all-important paperwork.'

'Indeed.'

Simnal strolled from the police station to St Leonard's Place. He checked his pigeonhole upon entering and found it contained just one item: an embossed, gold-edged card inviting him to a reception to mark the opening of a clinic of Psychology and Psychiatry in the Princess Alice Hospital in Hull. Simnal tapped the card on his hand. The date was convenient, and he needed to be known better, professionally speaking. His planned paper on 'the variable serial killer' would establish him as a leading light in the field of forensic psychology. He smiled. The invitation couldn't have come at a more opportune time.

Simnal and Ruth lay side by side in Simnal's bed, the sun streaming in through the open window.

'Hope I didn't make too much noise.' Ruth Day glanced at the open window.

Simnal grinned. 'It matters not.' He paused. 'Wednesday afternoons . . . sports afternoon throughout all England, and Scotland likewise.'

'And Wales. Don't forget the Taffys,' then she added in a Welsh accent, 'my grandfather Jones was Welsh, boyo . . . from Pontypridd, now.'

'Didn't know that.'

'Well you do now, boyo.' Then she said, 'And my grandfather Day, he was Irish, from Omagh . . . and my father was, still is, English, so there's tidy for you, bach.'

'Well, my grandfather Simnal is from Newcastle way, my mother's family have lived in the Vale of York since records began.'

Ruth stretched. 'Confess I'm getting quite fond of my Wednesday afternoon, "visits not coming back".'

'Social workers do this all the time, "visits not coming back" and spend the afternoon in the pub or at home watching the afternoon movie . . . that's why it's such a high stress occupation, you see.'

'I confess I did wonder.'

He glanced to his side. It's time you started making tracks.'

'Why? What time is it?'

'Four thirty.'

'Oh no!'

'See you tomorrow,' Simnal shouted after the frenzied, clothes-grabbing pink whirlwind as it dashed from his bedroom towards the bathroom.

'That's an original roof line,' Simnal followed the roofs of the terrace, 'all the buildings are of the same era . . . mid nineteenth century . . . interesting. I mean if you can ignore the cars on the street and the electric lamps, you're back in 1860 with that row of buildings.'

'Kippax on the Hill,' Ruth sniffed. 'It even looks bleak on a day like today. I can't begin to imagine what it would look like in the winter.'

'It is a bit exposed sitting atop of a hill.' Simnal glanced round. 'No one in the street at all. I've only ever seen this once before in Britain . . .'

'What?'

'A deserted street in a town in the middle of the day. It often seems to be the way of it in the USA. Driving through small towns there is often not a soul on the pavement, or sidewalk, as they say over there, but such is unusual in Britain.'

'Come to think of it, I don't think I have ever seen a street as deserted as this, in a town centre . . . the suburbs, yes, but not a town centre.' She turned to him. 'But you say you have?'

'In South Wales. When I was at Cardiff University I did a clinical placement at a hospital there, had to do a home visit to a small town near Merthyr Tydfil . . . I forget its name. I walked up the main street, it wasn't dissimilar to this, nineteenth-century brick buildings, grey slate roofs . . . except it wasn't on top of a hill, it was surrounded by them, you had to crane your neck to see the sky. I kid you not, there wasn't a soul to be seen, everything was still and quiet . . . nothing moved. I could have been looking at a photograph. This is only the second time in nearly thirty years that I have seen this . . . centre of a small town, middle of the day, a weekday, and not a living thing, human or animal, in sight.'

'I'll remember this, now you have pointed it out.' Ruth Day looked to her left and right up and down the narrow street of two-storey buildings, shops mostly, two pubs she could see, a cottage or two, a few parked cars, but only she and Simnal stood there. 'We passed a library back there . . .'

'Where?'

'Back that way.' She pointed to the Lawnmower Vendors and Repairs Service. 'Turn right at the end . . . it's on the left. They'll know where Westfield Road is. It's a Thursday, they'll be open. Library staff have Wednesday afternoons off . . . just like us.'

Simnal grinned. 'Well, I never . . . librarians . . . even librarians. Who'd have thought it?'

After obtaining directions from the library staff, 'First left . . . that's Westfield Road', Simnal halted his car outside a detached house of inter-war period and which was called 'Arreton'.

'It's on the Isle of Wight,' Kathleen Hood explained after Simnal commented on the name. 'It was named by the previous owner. He wouldn't explain it to us. He sold the house and went back to the south of England. We found out later that there is a village on the Isle of Wight called

107

Arreton. He might have named it after the village.' She was a large woman, big-boned, probably saw herself as being overweight, black shoulder-length hair which she centre-parted, heavy black-framed spectacles. She wore a loose-fitting white summer dress with a floral pattern, fleshy, naked legs ended in a pair of house shoes. Her house was neat, functional, yet Simnal thought it had a 'hard' quality about it, as though it lacked that woman's touch that can soften a home. Unusual, he thought, since Kathleen Hood lived alone. The rear room of her house in which she received Simnal and Day looked out on to a long, narrow and very well-tended garden, rich lawn, high privet and blooming flower beds, maintained by contract gardeners, Simnal assumed. Mrs Hood did not seem to him to be a woman with either the stamina or the inclination to keep on top of a garden of that size, with a potting shed, neatly varnished, at the bottom.

'Well,' Simnal said, 'as I said on the phone, we'd like to ask you a few questions.'

'And as I said, I'm here on my own all day every day since Eddie, my husband, walked out. No warning, nothing. I reported him missing.'

'You don't know where he is?'

'No. He'll be with his family in Castleford. There's no reason for him to be in touch, the house is mine, it was never even in joint names. It was me that had the pools win, not him . . . my crosses in the right boxes, not his. We lived here together, but it was my house, not his.'

'I see.' Simnal sat forward. 'You don't mind us asking you questions? We are psychologists, not police officers.'

'It's all right . . . it's your job, isn't it?'

'So long as your co-operation is freely given.'

'I'm curious about what you want to know.'

'Well, Dr Day here works at Kempton Hospital.'

'Ah . . . Humphrey.' Kathleen Hood smiled.

'Yes. And I visit Kempton Hospital weekly to talk to Mr

Sweet. Yes.' Kathleen Hood continued to smile as though the mention of Humphrey Sweet's name triggered a wealth of warm emotion. 'He has told me about you. Is this what you are here for? To talk about Humphrey?'

'No,' Simnal answered softly. 'We talk to Humphrey about Humphrey.'

'And his family. You talk to his family about him, he told me that you visited his parents.'

'Yes we did but that was a one-off, we won't be visiting them again. We will be talking to Humphrey again, though.'

'I see. So if it's not about Humphrey, what is it about?'

'Well . . .' Simnal glanced at Ruth Day, as if searching for help, 'we'd like to ask you about your friendship with Humphrey Sweet.'

'I visit him.'

'Yes, we know, for over a year now.'

'Yes.'

'The reason for our visit is that we want to know why.'

'Why I visit?'

'Yes. He's a multiple murderer. He's killed more people than he was convicted of killing.'

'I know, he's telling me . . . nothing more than he's told you. Each time I visit he says, "Kathleen, I've got something to tell you . . . I want you to hear it from me." He cares for me, you see.'

'How did you come to visit? Did you know him before he was arrested?'

'Oh, no.' Kathleen Hood shook her head vigorously as if offended that she should be thought to be the kind of woman who would associate with Humphrey Sweet when he was at liberty. 'I wrote to him as soon as I read that he had been sent to Kempton. I knew he was ill; he wasn't responsible for murdering those schoolgirls. So I wrote him a little note . . . not much . . . about as much as you could get on a postcard, but he wrote back. Never expected him

to write back but he did, such a kind letter, said things my
Eddie would never have said. I thought there was another
side to Humphrey Sweet that people don't see. There's
more than the ill man who couldn't stop himself murdering
those schoolgirls. He wasn't responsible for that, otherwise
they would have put him in prison. I mean, wouldn't they?
So I wrote back to him and he wrote back again and we
exchanged letters. Got to the point where we were
exchanging letters once a week, then I said I'd like to visit.
He said he'd love to see me, so I went. I mean, it's some
trek by public transport from here to Kempton. I start
early and get back late. Bus from here to Leeds, train
from Leeds to Hull, bus from Hull to the hospital and
they are not that frequent . . . leave here at eight . . . get
back about ten, eleven, twelve hours later. In the winter,
that's a long day.'

'I can imagine.'

'So I went. Nervous the first time, but he was so polite,
so well mannered, so softly spoken . . . a real gentleman
. . . asked about me. I knew then that I wanted to help him
in any way I could. He is portrayed as a monster, but he's
not. I know he's not. Just by visiting I am helping him.'

'Has he asked you to do things for him?'

'I bring him what I am allowed to bring him. It's a hospital
not a prison, but there are still restrictions on what you can
and cannot bring.'

'Any personal favours . . .?'

Kathleen Hood shot a glance at Simnal, paused, and then
said, 'No.'

'You don't find yourself doing things for him that you
don't want to do?' Ruth added, clearly seeing the trans-
parency of Kathleen Hood's denial. 'Things you don't want
to do, things you know are wrong but you find yourself
doing them anyway?'

'No.' No pause this time, but the denial was over strong.

'He has a charm about him,' Simnal said, 'there is no

denying that. I, we, are pleased for your friendship with Humphrey Sweet, as you say he is in hospital, the purpose is treatment, cure, and any positive relationship on the outside is a plus. It helps the patient, it helps the staff.'

Kathleen Hood smiled.

'But Mr Sweet has a dangerous personality, he's Jesuitical, in a word.'

'Jesuitical?'

'Plausible, cunning, crafty, sophistic.'

'He can manipulate people, Mrs Hood,' Ruth added.

'He's always so kind to me. In my life I have never known such kindness. Seemed I never had no one, just me and my mum when I was growing up. Couldn't get a man till Eddie came into my life then he left again. But I had Humphrey. Now you've come to tell me I shouldn't write to him. I'm all he's got. If I can help him I can do some good in my life. If it wasn't for Humphrey I would just slide through not doing nothing for me nor anyone else.'

'Well, just be careful. He has committed multiple murders, and despite how he presents to you, he, and people like him, can make people do things for him . . . he has a way of controlling.' Simnal spoke solemnly. 'Be careful. Do take my advice. Be careful.'

There was silence. Simnal stood. 'Well, thank you, Mrs Hood . . . that was interesting. Tell me, has Mr Sweet ever mentioned anybody called "Lenny" or "Alf" to you?'

'No.' Kathleen Hood shook her head vigorously. Too vigorously to seem truthful to Simnal and Day. 'Lenny? Alf? No, never.'

'Well, thank you, anyway.' Ruth also stood.

Driving away from Kippax, Simnal glanced at the clock on the dashboard of his car. 'Still only one p.m., and I have signed out for the day.'

'So have I.' Ruth turned and smiled at him. He responded. Their eyes met. 'So, grab some food at a Little Chef, then we could discuss this visit over tea in Hutton Cranswick.'

'Sounds good.'

After a pause Ruth Day said, 'On a more serious note, she lied to us. Not once, but twice.'

'I know.'

'Sweet's got her doing something for him she's unhappy about but didn't want to tell us about.'

'Well, I hope for her sake she's not getting in too deep. She didn't strike me as one who would survive easily in a woman's prison.'

'It's very interesting.' Nora Worth stirred her tea and glanced up at the green budgerigar in the cage by the window, 'it's very interesting, Poppet,' she said, in her soft voice. 'Never did like that woman since she moved in . . . something odd about her. Never saw her at all, did we, Poppet? Then her hubby disappears and she's always going out. Visiting someone . . . not going to the shops, never carries a bag . . . not a shopping bag, does she, Poppet? Just a handbag. She's got a fancy man, I think. Don't you, Poppet? She's too lively for a widow woman . . . and those two that visited just now, a man and a woman, they walked very close to each other when they went up her drive and when they left her house too. You saw, didn't you, Poppet? But they were not friends of Mrs Hood . . . that was an official visit. The police, possibly. We'll watch her, won't we, Poppet, you and me, like we watch all of Westfield Road, but we'll especially watch her.'

'They're called "death row groupies" in the United States.' Humphrey spoke before he sat down.

'Death row groupies?' Simnal raised an eyebrow.

'So I believe.' He sat. Still smiling. Very confident, thought Simnal. Very confident indeed.

'Who are?'

'People like Kathleen Hood whom you visited yesterday morning. She wrote me a letter immediately after you had left her. I received it this morning. "Visited by Drs Day and Simnal, wanting to know about us . . ." She said you were very nice and polite. She had that woman's-intuition impression that you two were an item. Well done. I just knew you were for each other.'

Simnal glared at Sweet.

'That reached home, didn't it?'

Simnal remained silent.

'Well . . . if two friends like you and me can't talk like that, who can?' This time, Sweet paused. 'I bet you are itching to tell me that you are not friends, aren't you? But you can't, in case I respond by breaking off all communication.'

Simnal held eye contact with him.

'And if I do that, you won't be able to study me, will you? You won't get to know about all the other bodies still to be found, will you? You need my co-operation more than I need yours, don't you? Anyway, Kathleen Hood is a death row groupie.'

'Death row groupie?' Again Simnal echoed the phrase.

'People . . . compulsive rescuers, who write to inmates on death row . . . or write to prisoners anyway . . . usually high profile prisoners . . . usually they are weak and needy people . . . the death row groupies, I mean.'

'And you would know that?'

'Well, it's my experience. Being in here. The letters I receive . . . they come from the Kathleen Hoods of this planet. I never have letters from people who have fulfilled lives . . . family men or women, or top and successful professionals . . . but from loners who write about their cars and dogs. As I said, people like Kathleen Hood. All alone since her husband left her. So she writes to me. Poor thing.'

'And you are not frightened of me telling her you think that about her?'

'No. Because you won't. Because if you do, I won't

speak to you . . . or to Dr Day. Then where will you be? No interesting research to do, and you and Dr Day won't have an excuse to be together. Where did you go after leaving Kathleen Hood's house, your place or hers? Had to have been your place, because she's trapped in a loveless marriage with a jealous husband.'

Simnal remained motionless, showing no emotion, holding eye contact with Humphrey Sweet, but his dislike, nay, his strong dislike for the man grew by the minute.

'So,' Sweet smiled, 'the Avon and Somerset police will be travelling north to interview me about young Mr Frost? That will be nice. I enjoy meeting new people. Helping the boys in blue. I'm told to help the boys in blue.'

'You are?'

'Yes. The voice inside my head. The voice that told me to go out and kill is now telling me to co-operate.'

'And of course with your co-operations your street cred grows. How is your standing in the world now that we all know about Mark Frost?'

'Getting better. It'll peak soon.'

'It will?'

'Yes. Because today's the day . . . today's the day I tell you about old Harry Carter.'

'That rings bells.'

'Rocks on the Dorset coast, near Poole. Perhaps you're thinking of them?'

'Yes,' Simnal smiled, 'perhaps I am. I have friends down that way; remember walking with them on the coast near Poole harbour. Yes, that was it, lovely summer's day . . . such a blue sea . . . I recall a Second World War pillbox perfectly preserved and free of graffiti. But it's another "old Harry" you are referring to.'

'Oh yes. Ever been to Rochdale, Lancashire?'

'No.'

'Well, you are not missing much. I used to rent a house there . . .'

'You did?'

'I did.'

'A little back-to-back . . . you know the type of house?'

'Yes.' Simnal nodded. 'Nice houses . . . very easy to keep warm and easy to secure against burglary having only one door, and one window at the street level . . . built in terraces, whole streets of them, soot black, all over the north of England.'

'That's the man.'

'So you rented one?'

'Yes. Used to drive over from York and spend the weekend in Rochdale. Always seemed to be raining. So I had a couple of spare rooms . . . sub-let them, just to see who'd come into my web.'

'You are going to tell me about another murder?'

'Is that a question?'

'Probably.' Simnal spoke slowly. 'Could equally be a statement. To tell you the truth, I'm not sure how I meant it.'

Sweet smiled. 'You're an honest man, Maurice . . . sorry, Dr Simnal. I like you. It would hurt me to hurt you.'

It was, thought Simnal, an odd thing to say, but he didn't comment.

'Well, quite a few took rooms but didn't stay. You have to be selective . . .'

'So you are telling me about another murder? You can call that a question.'

'Well in that case, yes, I am. Old Harry Carter. Nice old soul. Harry was perfect. All alone in the world. He would have been a good death row groupie . . . just him. Never went out, never received any post. Arrived with his worldly possessions in an old canvas holdall. Not like some, some had their friends help them move in, always went out, always received a lot of post.'

'They would be missed. Is that your point?'

'Yes.' Again Sweet smiled. 'Don't mind attacking folk

like that in the street, but when their place of residence can be linked to you, well then, you have to be careful. Then along came old Harry Carter, and not only was he alone in the world, but I hadn't done a disappearance . . . and I hadn't done a middle-aged one. Old Harry wasn't so old, not really. Not old like the old boy I did in his pensioner's flat. Not that old.'

'So tell me about old Harry.'

'Middle-aged guy, whiney voice . . . not difficult to see why he was on his own. A speaking voice that would drive a saint up the wall with irritation and his hard luck stories, poor little him . . . no skills to sell in the workplace.'

'So what did you do to him?'

'Banged him on the head. Planned it, though.'

'Oh, but of course.'

'One winter's night. You have to imagine it. Those black terraced houses with huge upright stone slabs dividing the back gardens, rain coming down, everybody snug in their little back-to-backs, and in our little back-to-back there was just me and whiney Harry, who was convinced he'd never had a chance in his life. He was sitting there, whining away with one eye on the television and I came up behind him with a hammer and wang! Over he went. That didn't kill him, he was semi-conscious. "What you doing, what you doing?" he said, but he was on the floor . . . couldn't get up, that's when I put the plastic bag over his head. That's killed him. Neat, I thought. I always thought that that would be the best way to kill someone. Bang 'em over the head, knock 'em out, plastic bag to finish the job. Neat and clean and silent. No mess to clear up. Need time though, that's the only obstacle, and privacy. But me . . . I had both. There was just me and him. No one called on us, no one we'd let in anyway, except the gas and electricity readers, but they don't call at weekends.'

'Weekend number was it?'

'Oh, yes. I was working at the dealership Monday to

Friday.' Sweet flashed a row of white teeth. 'Went over there one Friday evening, opened the door, Harry was there. "That you, Humphrey?" he said. "Glad you've come, I've been so lonely all week . . . no one to talk to. Shall we go out, Humphrey . . . have a pint in the pub? I'd like that, Humphrey . . ." about half an hour later he was dead, and all his little troubles were over.'

'What did you do with the body?'

'It's still there.'

'Still! How long has it been there?'

'About five years.'

'And no one's found it?' Simnal gasped.

'Well . . . it's in the cellar, isn't it? In the corner, under a pile of concrete but the concrete isn't coffin shaped. I folded old Harry's body up into a foetal position and let it solidify in that position . . . it gets hard. What's it called . . . rigor mortis? Then I punctured the stomach so the gases wouldn't build up.'

'Been doing your homework.'

'Watch true crime programmes on television. You learn a lot. All these guys who were caught because they made silly mistakes. One guy, he killed someone, weighted the body, I mean, really weighted it . . . and dumped it from a bridge into a deep river. End of story, he thought, but the build up of gas in the stomach was so great that it brought the body to the surface, despite the weight. So from that you learn to puncture the stomach. Even though I wasn't submerging it. Didn't know how the gases would react if it was enclosed in concrete, so I decided to release the gases. Made the house smell a bit, but I burned joss sticks and left the upstairs window open. Candles too.'

'Candles?'

'Yes. Candles on the stairs. See, the smell began to come from the cellar by Saturday evening, so I thought I'd better draw the air up from the cellar. So I put candles on the cellar steps, and on the stairs up to the top floor of the house and under the window I had opened. The convection created by all those candles drew the smell out of the cellar and out of the house. The windy weather helped as well, provided a good draught. Spent the Saturday buying candles by the dozen and a lot of cement powder. Did the last of the business on Sunday afternoon, late afternoon, early evening. Covered old Harry's body with cement powder and sprinkled it with water. It set quickly. Went back the next weekend and it was rock hard. Just a mound of cement in the corner of the cellar. The house was a long-term let . . . it's managed by a letting agency. Some person who bought it to let as a means of providing a pension for themselves, so I knew it would be some time before it was sold. Tenants wouldn't break up the mound of cement but new owners might. Nothing in the news about it, so that old property is still being rented, and old Harry's body is still where I put it. If anyone asked after old Harry I would say he left in the night. Came in the night and left in the night, owing money. I would have added that, just to make my story believable, but I needn't have worried, no one asked after him. No one noticed he had gone. Bit sad that. Gave up the tenancy a month later. Never knew much about him really. Hardly gave him a thought, unlike some of the others.'

'You'll recall the address, I assume?'

'Marshside.'

'Is that the name of the house?'

'No, it's the name of the street. No other word. Not Marshside Street, or Road, or Terrace, or Lane . . . nothing. Just Marshside, Rochdale. It's as bleak as it sounds. Number twenty-three. So that's the last resting place of poor, lonely, unloved and utterly unmissed Harry Carter: twenty-three, Marshside, Rochdale, Lancashire.'

'Interesting, you said you hadn't done a middle-aged one . . . so you were looking for different types of victims as well as using different methods to kill them.'

'Yes. I thought I'd made that plain.' Sweet looked to Simnal to be genuinely affronted.

'Just making the point . . .' Simnal explained. 'Just a point of clarification.'

'OK.' Sweet seemed satisfied. 'So I like 'em young, I like 'em old, I like 'em male, I like 'em female. Never did a little boy, though.'

Simnal froze.

'Never did that. I'd like a little boy. Had little girls, those schoolgirls . . . but never a boy. That's all I needed to make the list complete. Never starved anyone to death either. Or deprived them of water. Never did a really, really slow death.'

Maurice Simnal drove home, slowly, carefully. He felt nauseous, his legs weak. He let himself into his house, slumped into the chair by the telephone and phoned Tom Mautby. 'Dare say it could have waited until Monday, Tom,' he said, 'but the address is twenty-three Marshside, Rochdale.' He then gave Mautby an account of the death of one Harry Carter as related to him by Humphrey Sweet.

'Dare say it could have waited.' Mautby allowed himself to smile down the phone, knowing that a smile can be heard. 'Nothing for us to do, anyway, all I can do is relay this to the Lancashire boys. Spoil their weekend. Will you call in on Monday, dare say we'll have some feedback by then?'

'Will do.' Simnal replaced the phone. He dialled his wife. 'It's me,' he said.

'Oh.' Jane's voice, he thought, was a curious mixture of relief, gratitude, hostility and coldness.

'Is Toby there?'

'Not yet. On his way home from school, why?'

'Maybe nothing, but keep a close eye on him.'

'Why?' she replied with a clear note of alarm and Simnal imagined her face draining of colour, as he knew it would.

119

'If there's something I should know . . .'

'It's probably nothing.'

'Tell me!'

'A patient I am seeing . . . he's safely under lock and key . . . he might, might, might have made a threat against Toby.'

'Oh no . . .'

'But he's in a secure unit . . . Kempton . . . you don't get much more secure than that. More than that he's in the DSPD unit, the hospital within a hospital. He can't harm us.'

'He doesn't have to! These people have tentacles. They're called other people. How often have you remarked about the way psychiatric inpatients have a way of manipulating people? You know, people on the outside . . . getting them to do their dirty work for them!' she shouted, causing Simnal to move the phone away from his ear.

'He doesn't know where I live. Or you.'

'How do you know? It's the easiest thing in the world to find out where somebody lives. It's called following someone. It's called looking up their name in the phone book.'

'We're both ex-directory. It may be nothing. I shouldn't have phoned you.'

'No . . . no, you were right to phone me. I'll keep him close all weekend.' She paused. 'Who is your lady friend?'

'Just someone I met.'

'Toby took a shine to her. Is it serious?'

'Who knows . . . early days yet. We're not really off the ground.'

'Well, Toby didn't give that impression.' She had calmed, a note of indignation had replaced a note of alarm. 'Out of the mouth of babes came a clear picture of a very comfortable item, thank you very much. That's my bed she's stealing.'

'You still feel that it's your bed?' Simnal's heart leapt.

'Well, it was for long enough, until you made it impossible for me to stay. High powered, internationally famous psychiatrist, that's a lot of pulling power, but you can't pull with impunity. You can have your wife or you can have your little floozie . . . your bit on the side, but you can't have both. Oh . . .' she groaned. 'This is an old record . . . it's like a needle stuck in a groove. I'll keep him close by all weekend.' She slammed the phone down.

Simnal put the receiver down gently. His large house felt more empty than usual. 'What a mess,' he said to himself as he rose from his chair.

The realization that somebody had been in his house hit him like a battering ram. It wasn't like any of his burglaries. Property had been stolen, some valuable, some without any monetary value, but of immense personal value. He had been burgled before, and the cause must have been the same: he had left a window open in the summer evening to allow his house to breathe, believing that it was too high to climb into, and that no one would break into the front of a house in Hutton Cranswick, where nothing seems to go unnoticed. But he had reckoned, somewhat naïvely, given his occupation, he told himself, without the agility and the audacity of the cat burglar. It had been such a spiteful burglary too, his degree certificates, irreplaceable, but without value to anybody, old black and white family photographs, similarly of no value to anybody but himself and, in the fullness of time, Toby, all stolen. Along with more logical items like his expensive waterproof jacket, designed for the hill or the sea, but more often seen in wine bars, his dress watch, his bulging loose change jar, which he knew from experience contained about three hundred pounds. But this burglary was different, very different. In the first place, there was no sense that another person had been in his house. Before, there was a strong, inescapable sense that some person or persons unknown had been in his house. Over and above the damage and the loss, there was the real sense that someone had been in his house, he felt a strong sense at having been violated. In this case, the realization that someone had been in his house came slowly. In the second place, he had no sense that his house had been violated, there was no evidence of forced entry, valuable items were where he had left them, nothing at all seemed to be out of place, nothing, that is, until he went to the bathroom and found to his curiosity, before anything else, that a coffee mug, one of his, had been broken, and the pieces gathered together and placed neatly between the taps of the washbasin. He collected the broken pieces of clay and carried them down to the kitchen and to the waste bin beside the sink unit and there discovered that the clock in the kitchen was two hours fast. Simnal put the pieces of the coffee cup in the waste bin and then stood on a chair and took the clock off its peg on the wall and reset it to the correct time. If the clock was two hours slow then that could be explained by the battery having run its course, but to be advanced by two hours . . . that was the work of a human hand. Like the coffee mug, broken, taken upstairs in pieces, and the pieces neatly placed between the taps of the wash basin, absolutely midway between, to a centimetre, if not to a millimetre. Yet there was no sign of a break-in, no sign of forced entry.

Maurice Simnal sank slowly to the floor of the kitchen. He sat leaning against the cupboard doors. Who, he thought, could do this, who would want to intimidate him in this manner? Who would want to tell him that they could get into his house whenever they wanted to do so, and enter without having to use force? Only one person.

Sweet, Humphrey.

Courtesy of his 'tentacles'.

Six

Maurice Simnal passed a quiet weekend. It was also, he found, very uncomfortable. He was being intimidated. He could not protect his property. The unnerving feeling penetrated him to the core. His imagination began to overwork. He thought of the people dearest to him, Jane and Toby. He found that when he needed someone his thoughts turned to Jane, not Ruth. He missed her dreadfully, her scent, her voice, the way she moved, her warmth. He thought of the worst that they could do to him, and the worst he imagined was that they could murder Jane and Toby and cut off their heads and put the heads in the freezer in the cellar of his house. So fixated did he become with that fear that at three a.m. on the Saturday he lay in his bed, unable to sleep, straining his ears for every sound from outside and within his house, starting at every creak and rustling, and unable to prevent himself, he rose and went to the cellar to check the contents of the deep freeze. Finding it contained nothing except what he had put there, he returned to bed and sleep finally, mercifully, took him as dawn was breaking over the Wolds. He woke feeling on edge, reluctant to leave his house, but, having received a phone call from Ruth in which she regretted being unable to see him at all over the weekend because 'his lordship requires my presence', he determined to go out. To remain at home, he reasoned, was just giving in to them, whoever 'they' were. He also reasoned that he couldn't remain at home all the time, that at some point he would have to go out of doors and leave his house for an extended period. With that logic, he walked across the green at Hutton Cranswick and spent a pleasant two hours in the White Horse pub, sometimes standing alone at the bar, sometimes in friendly conversation with another villager. Upon his return home, and gratified to find that he had not been 'visited' in his absence, he felt a sense of victory. 'They' had not won, and he was reclaiming his territory. Sunday he passed quietly, mowing the lawn, weeding the flowerbed. Still a little agitated, but less so, so less so that he enjoyed a deep and uninterrupted sleep that evening and woke on the Monday feeling fresh and invigorated. On the Monday he drove to York, signed in at the Home Office building at St Leonard's Place and immediately signed out to 'the police' and walked to see Tom Mautby. Holding a mug of tea Mautby generously pressed on him, he related the intimidation he had experienced.

'I'd tell the local bobbies, if I were you,' Mautby replied after listening attentively.

'Really?'

'Yes. Report it. It's a crime. But you'll also do yourself a favour. If they can get into your house and adjust the clocks and break a coffee mug, they can get into your house and leave a stash of cocaine somewhere, or some other illegal substance, tip the police off anonymously, and they'll call, you will invite them in to look round because you believe you have nothing to hide . . .'

'And they find heroin or something . . . I see, hadn't thought of that. Yes, that would make things uncomfortable for me. I'll do that as soon as I can.'

'We can do it here, the sooner it's on record, the better. We can fax the statement to Driffield, for their information.'

'I'd appreciate that.' Simnal relaxed in the chair. 'Yes . . . I really would appreciate that.'

'Well, the Lancashire boys had an interesting but not a

pleasant weekend, just as you have had.' Mautby smiled.

'Really?'

'Yes, really.' He patted the phone on his desk with his meaty hand. 'Just had a call from them before you arrived. They found what you said they would find, and where you said they would find it.'

'Or where Humphrey Sweet said it would be. I was just the messenger.'

'Quite right. The Lancashire boys have managed to trace a relative.'

'Interesting. So Harry Carter wasn't as isolated as Sweet thought.'

'Apparently not. He had a brother known to the police, a few petty things, and Carter once reported him as a missing person. So they have a next of kin address. Over the weekend he provided a hair sample, they did a DNA match and got a result.'

'That was quick.'

'Well, it was a murder inquiry, it would have been given priority. Our forensic laboratory at Wetherby would do the same.'

'Yes, I dare say.'

'Harry was one of life's recluses. He wasn't alone in the world, it was more in the manner of him cutting himself off, but his brother was there when needed.'

'Strange how families fragment. Tragic too.'

'Indeed. Hope me and my brothers never lose contact like that.'

'Yes.'

'Do you have brothers?'

'Two.'

'Same here,' Mautby held eye contact with Simnal, 'and a sister.' He laughed. 'She got spoiled rotten. Three elder brothers . . . we were very protective towards her. Put any boyfriend well on his guard.'

'I can imagine.'

'Married a policeman. Daughter of a cop, two of her three brothers are cops, and she marries one.'

'What happened to the third brother?'

'That he's not a policeman you mean?'

'Yes.'

'Failed a medical. Defective hearing in one ear. He was badly cut up about it. Became a teacher, over-stressed and underpaid. So he says.'

'One of my brothers achieved a childhood ambition and became a train driver.' Simnal smiled. 'The other is a career soldier.'

'Really?'

'Well, RAF.'

'Pilot?'

'Good Lord, no. Sergeant in the RAF Regiment. He's set to spend his working life guarding airfields. He'll get a reasonable pension at the end of it all, I expect, and he's seen some interesting parts of the world, and he'll see more before he's done.'

'So you broke the mould and made it to university?'

'To the delight of our parents, yes.'

'Anyway . . . Sweet, the Lancashire police want to interview him now, the Avon and Somerset boys are coming up this week. The Lancashire boys have agreed to wait until they have interviewed him about that young student he stabbed.'

'He's right . . . Sweet is correct. Who on earth would have connected the murder of a student in Bristol, stabbed and left in open ground, in a posh area, with the murder of a middle-aged loner in down-at-heel Rochdale, who was suffocated and buried under a pile of concrete in the cellar of a terraced house?'

'No one.'

'No reason to believe they were connected, but Sweet wants his kudos, and we now connect them.'

'Will you mention the intimidation when you see him again?'

'Don't think so. Don't want him to have a victory if it is him who is behind it. I'll talk to Ruth Day, see what she thinks, but my inclination is not to tell him.'

'So . . .' Mautby stood, 'let's go and take your statement. The statement forms are downstairs.'

'Thanks.' Mautby took hold of the file. 'It's just a notion, you see. They've paid dividends before.'

'Certainly have.' DS Jimmy Dancer turned towards the door. 'I'll leave you with it, I'm next door if you need me or for when you've finished.'

After taking Simnal's statement and filing a copy to the police at Driffield for their information, Mautby had returned to his office and pondered upon what Simnal had told him about Kathleen Hood, and especially upon her missing husband, Edward 'Eddie' Hood. Ordinarily he wouldn't give a second thought to the news of a man who had gone missing some years earlier: it was the responsibility of another police force and, sadly, people do go missing. Two things, however, bothered him about the disappearance of Eddie Hood, things that Maurice Simnal as a psychologist clearly didn't pick up on, but Mautby as a police officer did. First was Hood's age. Simnal didn't mention Mrs Hood's age, but he gave the impression of a person in her middle years, whose husband would presumably be of the same age group. Not, he knew, an age when people tend to go missing. That in itself was curious. Secondly was the overall context of the report of Eddie Hood's disappearance, the context being a litany of murder; Sandy Sheenan, battered and his body buried close to another lake in Scotland; Edward Stamner, another Edward by coincidence, also battered but left in his pensioner's flat; Mark Frost, whose life must have stretched endlessly before him as he walked his last walk in life, just in the wrong place at the wrong time, who was stabbed and left in open view in a residential area of Bristol; Harry

Carter, who had isolated himself from his kith and kin and whose body was found in a cellar in a house in Rochdale, Lancashire, covered in concrete. And now a person is reported missing. There was no suggestion that Humphrey Sweet was involved in Eddie Hood's disappearance, but he was there, in the background. There was a connection. Mrs Hood, wife of a missing man, is a regular visitor to the man who clearly had murdered three schoolgirls, Sandy Sheenan, Edward Stamner, Mark Frost, Harry Carter, and heaven knows how many more. To Tom Mautby, sitting in his office, it had all suddenly smelled like an open sewer on a hot day.

On a very hot day.

He had picked up the phone and phoned the West Yorkshire police and had ascertained from a female officer, with a warm and friendly telephone manner, that the interested police officer was Detective Sergeant James Dancer 'out at Castleford'. A second phone call had further ascertained that DS Dancer was indeed on duty that afternoon and wasn't expected to be leaving his office . . . 'not with this pile of paperwork in front of me'. One hour later Tom Mautby was sitting in front of James 'call me Jimmy' Dancer, explaining his interest in the disappearance of Edward Hood. Jimmy Dancer proved to be a tall, lean officer, young for DS rank, thought Mautby, and whom he found to be with a ready smile and keen wit. He handed Mautby the file on Edward Hood.

'It's just a notion, you see,' said Mautby, 'they've paid dividends before.'

Mautby read the file. It took a matter of minutes. It really contained nothing more than the details provided by Mrs Hood and a photograph of Mr Hood, who seemed a round-faced man who wore black-framed spectacles, had closely cut black hair, a narrow nose and thin lips. He looked to Mautby to be an unimaginative man, dull of spirit, parochial of viewpoint. Not, he thought, a person likely to disappear, not a man who would want to walk out of an old life into a new one, not a man to rub shoulders with the criminal fraternity and be buried in a shallow grave. It seemed to Mautby that Edward Hood's day-to-day world would have been encompassed by the distance from his house to Kippax Main Street, and his idea of a trek would have been the bus ride to the coast. An open sewer on a hot day.

Mrs Hood had reported her husband as being missing some two years earlier. The duty constable noted her manner seemed 'calm and unconcerned'. And that was that. Just another missing person, one of the two hundred thousand who are reported missing every year in the UK. In fairness, thought Mautby, there was nothing else the West Yorkshire police could do. They had followed up Mrs Hood's report by visiting her at home, as procedure dictated, and the visiting police officer, DS J. Dancer, had also recorded how strangely unconcerned seemed Mrs Hood. Mautby closed the file, carried it to the next room and tapped on the doorframe.

'Come and take a pew.' Jimmy Dancer smiled. 'Come in. Didn't take you long. Didn't think it would.'

Mautby sat in front of Dancer's desk.

'It's a very thin file. Not like these.' Dancer patted the pile of files on his desk.

The window behind him looked out on to the centre of Castleford and it was not to Mautby's taste: low-rise nineteenth-century buildings, narrow streets and one or two empty shop units. Not a prosperous town, assuming the town's economy had declined with the coal industry in the late twentieth century. 'I see,' Mautby said. 'Not much else you could do, though.'

'Well, as you see, nothing points to foul play, and he's well over the age of sixteen.'

'What do his relatives say?'

'As I recall, they do suspect foul play . . . don't know where he is.'

'You didn't take statements from them?'

'No. They had no information.'

'I see. Maurice Simnal . . .'

'Who?'

'A forensic psychologist who visited Mrs Hood in connection with a patient of his . . . he and I are working on the case of Humphrey Sweet.'

'The murdered schoolgirls . . . just sat there waiting to be arrested with the body of one of the girls in his arms. One weird sicko . . . Where is he?'

'Kempton.'

'Doesn't surprise me.' Dancer leaned back in his chair, and in doing so revealed more of Castleford's rooftops to Mautby's view, who thought the town must be the horse's rump in winter if on a day like that, hot and with a near cloudless blue sky, it looked as bleak as it managed to look.

'Well, there's questions about his sanity. Or should I say questions about his insanity.'

'What! You mean they think he's sane? You astound me.'

'Well . . . apparently his personality is just not breaking down, as it would be expected to break down after this length of time, but he's doing what he can to convince the authorities that he's insane, because Kempton is a soft bed compared to E-Wing Durham, which is where he'll go if they think he's sane. But the nurses are convinced he's sane, so I am told. The doctors are hedging their bets. He's disclosing more murders.'

'More!'

'Yes. You'll hear about it. He is one prolific serial killer.'

'Blimey.' Colour drained from Dancer's face.

'He wants the kudos, the acclaim, the infamy.'

'Sounds a suitable case for treatment to me.'

Mautby opened his palms. 'Not for you and me to say, really.'

'As you say,' Dancer nodded in agreement. 'Not indeed

for little us to say. And the connection with Edward Hood
is . . .?'

'Mrs Hood is a regular visitor to Humphrey Sweet.'

'Really!'

'Yes, really, and given Sweet's ability to control people
. . . it places a cloud of suspicion over Edward Hood's
disappearance.'

'You think she murdered him, on Sweet's orders?'

'I don't think anything at the moment. I am just probing
to see where I get. But she did start visiting him before her
husband disappeared.'

'That is interesting.'

'So I'd like to talk to her relatives.'

'Their addresses are in the file. I'd like to accompany
you if you don't mind.'

'What about your paperwork?'

'That can wait.' Dancer stood and reached for his jacket.
'For this, that can wait.'

Maurice Simnal drove to Hull. He didn't relish the thought
of the reception to mark the opening of the new Psychology
department at the Princess Alice Hospital; he had never
been a party animal. Even in youth a quiet evening in a
pub with a couple of good friends had always seemed to
him to be far, far preferable to a riotous party. It was protocol
and his career advancement which made his attendance a
necessity. He could not, for his own sake, fail to attend,
though he resolved as he drove across the flat East Yorkshire
countryside with the car window wound down and listening
to soothing Radio Four, that his attendance would be brief.
He would be seen, he would talk to the people he had to
talk to and then quietly slip away, and home early.

He parked in the hospital car park, entered the building
and asked directions at the porter's lodge. Following directions given by a full-faced jovial porter, he found the new
department which had in fact, he found, been up and running

for fully six months, though it still smelled new with clean, unworn carpets. Vases of flowers proclaimed the day to be special. The guests he saw were many and varied, from eminent physicians in suits to a man wearing a mayoral chain of office. He gave his name at the reception and was handed his name badge which he loosely attached to his lapel. It was, after all, not going to be on very long. He entered the reception which was held in the foyer of the building, took a glass of white wine and a sausage on a stick and looked around for a friendly face amid the hubbub of conversation.

'Good afternoon, Dr Simnal.' The friendly face that found him belonged to a middle-aged lady, whose name by her badge was Betty Miles, and by her designation, the deputy in charge of the new unit. 'Thank you for coming.'

'Delighted to be here.' Simnal smiled.

'Do you know anybody here?'

''Fraid not.' Simnal continued to smile. 'I work for the Home Office, I don't know many psychologists in Health Authority employment. Probably about time I met someone.'

'Well, let's see.' Betty Miles turned and scanned the room. 'Well, there's Daniel . . . I'll introduce you.' She cupped her hand gently around Simnal's elbow and guided him across the room to where three men stood in affable conversation.

'Excuse me,' Betty Miles interrupted the conversation. 'Can I introduce Dr Simnal, he's a psychologist. This is Dr Daniel Ireland, the most senior psychologist in this Area Health Authority.' Simnal and Ireland shook hands and said 'hello' to each other. Ireland was a tall man in his fifties who had a missing left canine, which he was clearly content to live without rather than compensate with false teeth.

'Pleased to meet you, sir,' Simnal added, thinking that Dr Ireland was exactly the sort of person that he needed to meet.

'Dr Simnal is employed by the Home Office,' Betty Miles explained. 'He doesn't know many of us Local Health Authority types. Oh, please excuse me, there's somebody I must talk to.' She turned on her heels and walked away leaving Simnal with Ireland and the other two men.

'So,' Ireland said, 'Home Office. You're a forensic psychologist I assume?'

'Yes. I'm working on a Government-funded project at the moment, trying to identify early characteristics of people who go on to become serial killers . . . catch them before they start.'

'Ethically questionable,' Ireland observed in a non-aggressive way. 'Not your work, I mean, can't see anything immoral there, but if we do identify someone who has all the potential to be a multiple murderer, do we lock him up before he kills, or wait until he does kill?'

'Well, that's the issue, isn't it,' Simnal replied. 'I personally tend to the belief that a person has to be proven dangerous before he's locked up, even if that means he murders someone.'

'Brave stance.' Ireland inclined his head.

'Well, the alternative is locking someone up, often for life, because they are deemed dangerous, and if that system works, it has to be right all the time. If just one person is deprived of his liberty, especially for an extended period, as a result of a misdiagnosis, then the entire system fails.'

'Yes,' Ireland nodded.

'But I would see any findings of my research being used to identify serial killers in the making, while they're still children, time to turn them around. Means they don't kill anyone, and they don't spend any unnecessary time in gaol. I can live with that. Children who demonstrate acts of cruelty, for example, they should be flagged up and interceded with, like Brady and his cat.'

'Who and his cat?' The question was asked by an olive-skinned man.

'Ian Brady . . .' Simnal spluttered as he read the man's name badge. His heart thumped. The questioner was one Abdul Bashir. 'He and Hindley committed the Moors murders in the early 1960s.'

'Oh yes,' Bashir nodded, 'terrible business. Brady had a cat, you say?'

'Not as a pet. The story is that when he was growing up in Glasgow . . .'

'Splendid city,' offered the fourth man, Dr Thackery, by his name badge, surgeon. 'Badly – unfairly maligned.'

'Indeed.' Simnal struggled to remain calm. 'But the story is that when Brady was a youngster, of school age, he kept a cat trapped in a hole in the ground, put a large stone over it, and he would check on the cat each day until it died of thirst or starvation. Whether that is true or not I don't know, but if children who do similar things are reported instead of being merely remonstrated with, then we could work with them before they become old enough and strong enough to take human victims. That makes the project worthy, I would say.'

'Indeed,' Ireland smiled, 'since you explain it thusly.'

'Where are you interviewing?' Dr Bashir asked, in a perfect English accent, which surprised Simnal.

'Various hospitals in the Yorkshire and Humberside area. Kempton most recently, though my work has got a little side-tracked there . . . opened out into unexpected areas in respect of one particular patient.'

'Kempton? You'll probably have met my wife. Dr Day, psychologist Dr Day. I am a medical doctor, I work here at the Princess Alice.'

'Yes . . . I do, yes. Dr Day, yes we are working closely with the particular patient I mentioned. I'm sorry I didn't realize you were her husband . . . the name . . .' Simnal struggled to remain calm. He fought the urge to take flight.

'Ah,' Bashir smiled warmly, 'that is Ruth. She is very headstrong and refuses to take my family name as her married name, much to the chagrin of my father. He's still very conservative in such matters. He's anxious to have his grandchildren as well and Ruth is dragging her feet there too. So the relationship between father-in-law and daughter-in-law is frosty.'

'Your English is very good, I feel bound to say . . . accent is flawless.'

Bashir laughed, as did Miles and Thackery.

'It ought to be,' Thackery explained, 'he's one of us.'

'I do beg your pardon.' Simnal struggled, feeling more and more uncomfortable by the second.

'Not to worry. The name and the Mediterranean look is misleading. My grandfather was an Egyptian merchant seaman. Didn't know which way was the centre of Hull, found he was waiting on the wrong side of the road, no time left to go into town before the pubs chucked 'em out, didn't particularly want to go back to the ship, so he walked into a pub that was close by the bus stop, the barmaid that served him became my grandmother. If he had been waiting on the correct side of the road they wouldn't have met and he would have returned to Egypt. Anyway, they fell for each other very rapidly and he jumped ship to stay with her.'

'Really . . .?' Simnal smiled in approval of the story, but his scalp was beginning to crawl.

'Yes. They married, took a shop in east Hull. He was self-supporting so the authorities let him stay. Today he would have been given "indefinite leave to remain" after two years of marriage to an English woman, but not in those days. He spent the greater part of his life in England but lived and died a "foreign national". My father, also Abdul like my grandfather, was born above the shop in east Hull and he won a scholarship to Hull Grammar and read medicine at Sheffield University and the mould was broken. I was born in Hull in more favourable circumstances than my father, and followed him into medicine, though I am a surgeon, he is a general practitioner. So I am Abdul Bashir the third.'

'And a very proper Englishman,' Thackery added. 'Very pukka.'

'But equally proud of my Egyptian heritage.' Bashir's chest seemed to swell. 'My father took me to Cairo to meet our family when I was a boy . . . a few times in fact. And when Ruth is prepared to put motherhood before her career I hope to be able to do the same with my son. But while Ruth keeps saying "there's still time" I have to be patient. Do you have children, Dr Simnal?'

'A boy, sir. He's seven.'

'You are a lucky man.'

'Yes, I feel I am.' Simnal's voice faltered. 'I am indeed fortunate. But yours is an interesting story. Very interesting.'

'Yes, it's good for cocktails, breaks the ice. But I envy you your son. I look forward to taking my son sailing, well, boating . . .'

'A yacht, Dr Bashir?' Simnal asked. 'You have a yacht?'

'No . . . a motor launch. *Free Radical*. It's a medical term, as you'll know. Just a little one. Keep her in Hull Marina and turn west. Take her up river under the bridge, sometimes anchor, or moor up for the night, and return the following day but wouldn't take her out of the estuary. She's not a sea boat.'

'I see.' Simnal sipped the last of his wine. 'I see. I wonder, would you gentlemen please excuse me . . . I . . . er . . . if you'd excuse me.'

'Never did like that woman.' Ralph Hood glanced out of the window of his small council-owned property in Castleford. Mautby followed his gaze and saw a blue tit hanging upside down on a string bag of nuts pecking at the contents. The garden in which he and Dancer stood was kept neatly, Mautby noticed, a close-clipped hedge, an equally close-cut lawn, a flowerbed without a trace of a weed. Beyond were the backs and roofs of houses in the adjacent street. Ralph Hood turned to Mautby. 'You're looking at my garden?'

'Yes.' Mautby smiled. 'I was listening to you, of course, sir, but having a garden myself I can tell the amount of work you put into yours.'

'Aye. Well now the coal's gone there's not a lot else to do for a man of my years. Thirty years underground and then the dole. Too old to retrain, see, just the garden now. Healthier, like, but the money's no good.' He laughed at his own joke. He was a short, barrel-chested man, who wore a scarlet shirt and brown corduroy trousers. His feet were encased in blue carpet slippers.

Mautby grinned. He decided he liked Ralph Hood. 'I gather they were not long married?'

'No. A few years. Both middle-aged when they met, the marriage puzzled me, puzzled all of us, really. Our Edward, our Eddie, he was a man who seemed happy with the single life. He was a pitman like me, got laid off like me when the coal failed, but me, I like home comforts; I like a woman in the house. You'll never fathom a woman, change their minds like you and me change our socks, but they do soften a house. I used to love coming home from the pit after a morning shift on a winter's day to a lovely clean and warm house with the smell of home cooking coming from the kitchen. I took to marriage very well but then, I had a good 'un. Our Meg was a treasure. She was a pitman's daughter so she understood a pitman's life, she understood what a pitman wants and needs. A calm tidy house to come home to, and a solid meal on the table, piping hot, especially on a winter's night. Then it were down to the miners' welfare for a few pots from about six till nine, then an early night for to be up for the six a.m. shift. Hardly ever saw daylight in winter. That's her.' Ralph Hood pointed to a framed photograph of a middle-aged woman with a warm

smile, which stood on the mantelpiece. 'Lovely lass. She
went sudden, like, two years ago.'

'Sorry.'

'Aye, well, I gave her a good life so I don't feel guilty
about anything. I brought home the money, we never went
hungry, two weeks at the coast each year, Bridlington one
year, Scarborough the next, turn and turn about, see. She
had the house, I had the garden. What more could any
woman want? Well now it's me daughter, she lives on the
next street her and her husband, but she comes round twice
a day and does for me, and each day I go round to their
house for my supper, so I still get fed, but our Eddie, he
seemed well content to go home to an empty house. I mean
no welcome at all, and then to cook for himself and that's
after hewing six foot of coal, eight hours on your side and
we worked in a wet seam, making six feet a shift. That's
hard graft.'

'Thought it was done by machines?' Tom Mautby asked.

'Big wide seams, aye but not where me and Eddie worked.
That was a narrow seam. Pick and shovel work. But Eddie
seemed happy enough, always looked like a bachelor,
buttons missing from his shirt, shirts never ironed, he'd
wear a suit until it shone with age and was set to fall apart
while it was on him. Our Meg would never let me go out
looking like that. Then he brings her to the miners' welfare,
doesn't he? So she lives in a bought house in Kippax, not
a council house in Castleford, but what a dull woman, hardly
any spark, hadn't got no "give". See what I mean . . . you'd
give to her, talk to her, but you'd get nowt back. Like she
was brain dead. But Eddie was having his way and they
wed at Castleford Registry Office. Cloudy day and it rained,
and our Meg said that it was a bad sign . . . a bad omen,
she said, and wasn't she right. Not long wed and Eddie
disappears.' Ralph Hood put his hand to his forehead.
'Vanishes. It's bad, that. It'd be better if we knew he was
dead, like our Meg, we'd have a grave to visit when the

weather's good.' He glanced at the window again. 'Aye, if this weather holds I'll be up the cemetery tomorrow, take a bunch of flowers from the garden, talk to the headstone like I was daft . . . you know, soft in the head, away with the little folk, but it's like that up there, a whole line of people talking to gravestones. But with Eddie you can't do that.'

'So what do you think happened?' Jimmy Dancer brought the conversation back to the matter in question.

Ralph shrugged. 'I can tell you what I don't think happened, I can tell you that our Eddie wouldn't have walked out on that woman and walked into a new life. For one, he wouldn't have the savvy, for two, he was too old, for three, he'd hardly been ten miles from Castleford in his days, and for four, he wouldn't walk out on his family. The Hoods are a big family among the miners of this town, we've got a good name, seven of us brothers and sisters, Harry, Tom, me, Stanley, then it were our Eddie, then the girls, Mary and Edith. Hardly a year between each one, and our mother, she was one of those women that liked being pregnant, said it made her feel like a contented cow. Our dad always said he'd had enough after four, but our mother insisted. We grew up close, all married except Eddie and he did eventually, and all settled in Castleford. That's a family with strong bonds, Mr Dancer. Troubled teenagers leave home and vanish, so do women in bad marriages. I mean Eddie's marriage wasn't bad, but it was a bit lifeless, seemed to me, anyway. That woman couldn't have held me in a state of wedlock, and if Eddie wanted to walk out on her he would have come back to Castleford, with us, his kin. Close family we are. See, that's why I think some badness has happened to our Eddie. He'll be lying on the moor some-where with grass growing through his bones, poor lad. And it's not knowing, like I said, that's the worst of it.'

'What do you know about Mrs Hood? How did they meet?'

Ralph Hood inclined his head to one side. 'You know, I never knew how they met. One day he was single, fancy-free, next he was getting married. She just appeared. She isn't local, not a Castleford lass, maiden name was Partridge, daft name, but it was a good name for her . . . partridge in a pear tree, because she was cuckoo once. So Eddie said.'

'Cuckoo?'

'Mad. Sick in the head. Was in hospital, that big one, north of Leeds. I think it's closed now, or is closing, High Royds. She was in there getting her head seen to. Explains a lot, explains why she's not bothered about our Eddie, she's not with us, don't know where she is, but it's not this planet. Used to call on her a few times after Eddie vanished, she would be sitting there. Just blinking, never offered me a cup of tea or anything. Not bothered about our Eddie. No worry about him at all.'

'Kathleen Partridge you say.' Jimmy Dancer opened his notebook. 'Known to High Royds. "Partridge", as in a pear tree . . .'

'So you're doing something at last?'

'We're not searching for him. I explained that when he went missing, we can't search for adults.'

'Let's just say that there may have been developments.' Tom Mautby explained. 'Can't say anything further. Not yet.'

Simnal walked around the perimeter of the green at Hutton Cranswick. He realized that in his life he had never been betrayed until he met Ruth Day. Meeting her again was going to be difficult. Should he tell her that he had met her husband, tell her that her tale of the state of her marriage to a man who just wants 'indefinite leave to remain' stamped on his passport was a tissue of lies? How could he continue to work with her? How was anything else between him and her at all possible? He felt nauseous; there was a weight in his stomach. He had lost his appetite; he had lost his will, his enthusiasm. He glanced up at the sky, vast and blue, and thought how apparently small the great dome made him feel. How purposeless was life if one felt one had no part in it. He returned home and phoned his wife on her mobile, still his wife . . . She answered. He heard the sound of a car in motion in the background. He looked up at the wall-mounted clock, 15:30 hours. She'd be driving to meet Toby from school, rushed as usual, he thought, and pictured her with the mobile phone illegally pressed to one ear while driving the car. He would keep this short. He realized he shouldn't have phoned her; he had placed her in danger. 'It's me . . .' he said. He heard an unintentionally apologetic tone in his voice.

'What is it? I'm busy.'

'Yes . . . sorry. I just need to tell you that I am sorry.'

There was no reply. Just a stunned silence and beyond, the sound of the car.

'I've just found out what you must have felt,' he continued. 'What you must be feeling.'

'What is this?' His wife was incredulous.

'I knew I was wrong . . .'

'I'll say!'

'But I never knew the depth of the emotion you must have felt, until today. I am so sorry.'

'Ha!' The laugh was sharp and joyful. 'Your lady friend has been playing away from home. Well, there's justice, there's justice for you. So it's true, what goes around comes around, the notion of karma is true after all. Well, this has made my day. I'm going to sleep well tonight. I'll see you at the weekend on crowded Lendal Bridge unless you've thought of a better place yet?'

'No . . . I just wanted to tell you, I am so sorry.'

'Well, you've told me!' She switched the phone off.

Seven

Simnal thought Humphrey Sweet looked more smug than he usually did.

'I have come to look forward to our little chats, Maurice.'

'Dr Simnal. I have told you.'

'Ah.' He held up a defensive hand. 'I am so sorry. Unfortunately I fear that this will be the last but one.'

'Oh?'

'Well, just two more murders to report. The police have visited me,' Sweet announced proudly.

'I'm not surprised.'

'Well, all those little murders . . . they were very polite. Dare say it helps their conviction rate.'

Simnal looked behind Sweet. Through the pane of glass he could see the ward with its tall windows and high ceiling, the nurses, the patients, some lying on their beds, some grouped round the television, some shuffling disconsolately down the ward, all dressed in casual day clothing, all looking like normal humans, people who wouldn't merit a second glance if they were passed on the street, yet all residents of the DSPD, twenty patients, among them responsible for nearly one hundred murders. 'They've charged you?'

'Oh yes. Had to. The formality, you see. Won't make a deal of difference to me. They won't send me for trial, Maurice . . . sorry, Dr Simnal. I mean how can they, not guilty by reason of insanity? I might get moved from here, but I'll be in the hospital system.'

'Which is what you want?'

'Preferable to gaol, Dr Simnal.' Sweet smiled. 'I'm getting to be cock of the walk now.' He indicated the ward behind him. 'Reckon this will do it for me, these two.'

'Two?'

'One today, one next week. Then we won't see each other again.'

'We won't?'

'Well, no point, is there?'

'Well, I might want to go into greater depth with you, Humphrey.'

'Greater depth?'

'I do have a brief which is other than facilitating your confession to a series of murders. This has been quite superficial, just getting to know each other. I really have to find out what makes you tick. I want to know about your childhood.'

'You know about it. You visited my parents. You found out that I killed animals, little defenceless furry animals. And fish. The goldfish, remember.'

'Yes. That's the area I really want to go into.'

'But I might not want to go into it.'

'Or your first act of violence towards another person.'

'Me and some friends tried to derail a train once. Didn't succeed. Would have been good. Put a bit of metal on the northbound track, got the time right, on the East Coast mainline, in front of an express . . . reckoned without the southbound express, didn't we? Thundered past, saw us, saw the obstacle, radioed his control and they stopped the northbound express. Made a big splash in the papers. The driver of the southbound express gave a good description of us, even though he saw us for only a few seconds. We kept low after that, the police were looking for us.'

Simnal looked at Sweet in an interested manner. This was the sort of thing he was looking for. The confessions to the murders was of huge importance, but it added little to his research. This, on the other hand, was gold dust. 'How old were you?'

'Fourteen.'

The answer surprised Simnal. Sweet was younger than he had expected him to have been. 'You escaped detection, how?'

'Well, kept our heads down. Didn't go around together in public for a while. Also, cops were too locally focused, we travelled fifteen miles to do that.'

'That is a long way for fourteen-year-olds.'

'Travelled by bus, walked the rest of the way to the railway line, the Doncaster to York section. Police were looking for local lads, never occurred to them that fourteen-year-olds from as far away as Selby would do that. So we were safe. It's one of the first things you learn, Dr Simnal. Never soil your own nest.'

That too was an observed pattern. The more serious the crime, the further the perpetrator will live from the crime scene. A vandal will not throw stones at a neighbour's greenhouse, but at a greenhouse two streets away; a burglar will not turn windows in the area of the town where he lives, but will go to adjacent areas; a serial murderer will trawl for victims in towns other than the one in which he lives. 'Was that a planned decision, to go far away?'

'Instinctive really,' Sweet said matter-of-factly, 'and because that's where the fast tracks are. Couldn't derail a train near Selby, they go too slow. You need speed for a successful derailing. So Donald said. And we didn't want to soil our own nest, like I said.'

'Donald?'

'One of us.'

'What happened to your friends later?'

'Lost contact. I heard Donald got himself known to the law and Tiny . . . well, Tiny is the law. He became a policeman, so I heard.'

'Tiny?'

'His name, on account of his size. A joke. He was a big boy. You could see why the police took him.'

'Donald and "Tiny",' Simnal repeated. 'When you were fourteen.'

Sweet smiled. 'Won't do you any good.'

'What won't?'

'Telling the cops about Donald and Tiny.'

'Oh?'

''Cos they're not their real names, I made them up. You don't grass on your mates. Tiny was a big lad, and he might have joined the fire service . . . see . . . I'm smudging it a bit, but the incident did happen. You can check.'

'I will.'

'I'll get charged with that as well. All feathers in my cap.'

'Any other attacks on persons?'

'A few. Some more successful than others.'

'Such as?'

'Such as no more, because this helps you, not me. Today I want to tell you about the girl.'

'The girl?'

'Noticed anything about my victims, Dr Simnal?'

'They are all different in some way, age, social class, but that's what you intended.'

'And all male.'

'Yes, until you murdered the three schoolgirls.'

'No . . . had females before. Two. And both in rural areas. Got away from the town for the women. A little more confusion for the boys in blue to contend with.'

'So tell me.'

'Found out later she was called Geraldine Toovey.'

'Geraldine Toovey.'

'Yep. It was a nice one.'

'How?'

'Opportunistic. Just fell into my lap, almost literally. And she was dead within sixty seconds of my meeting her. I was

trawling across in the Halifax area, maybe into Huddersfield
. . . you know that area, those little mill towns all blend into
each other. It was a dark rainy evening, when . . . four, five
years ago . . . just outside the town centre, picked her up in
the car headlights, walking angrily . . . you know, a heavy
footfall like she'd just found out her boyfriend or husband
was having an affair with another woman.'

Simnal eyed Sweet coldly. Was the man shooting in the
dark, or did he even know about Miss Clark? He remained
expressionless and did not comment, he wasn't going to
feed Sweet anything.

'I was going to drive past, but lo and behold, didn't she
flag me down? She must have thought I was a minicab, in
fact she did, because she opened the door and said, 'Are
you for hire?' I said, 'Yes love, where to?' She got in out
of the rain; my right hand went into my right pocket for
the stiletto I carried. It's not a proper knife, it's a letter
opener, thin, eight-inch blade, sharply pointed tip, but
perfect for the job I had in mind. She sat in the car, pulled
the door shut, wet as a drowned rat. You know how it can
rain in those Pennine towns in winter. She gave a cry of
alarm as she realized she hadn't got into a minicab and then
I plunged the letter opener into her side, just above her hip.
That didn't kill her but she wasn't going to escape after
that, left the letter opener in her side and snapped her neck.
It's easy if you know how. No cars about, no one on the
street because of the rain, could have been in the middle
of a desert for all the witnesses there were. Drove her
towards Manchester. Turned up a side road, turned up
another side road, well into rural areas by this time, wind-
swept moorland. You know the type.'

'Yes.'

'You've walked that sort of country?'

'Yes.'

'You look the walking type.' Sweet smiled, as if drawing
Simnal to him.

'I do?' Simnal remained stern-faced.

'You have strong legs. There's a lot of strength in your legs, but not much in your upper body.'

'You can tell, can you?'

'Yes, by the way you move. I think I could beat you at arm wrestling, but I'd tire on a hike before you would.'

'We'll never find out if either is true, but carry on . . . don't interrupt your delivery.' Simnal spoke solemnly.

'I pulled the car up, took her handbag, went through the contents, that's how I found her name. Took her cash, about twenty pounds, put that in my own pocket, paid for my petrol home. Then I removed all her clothing, put each item in the rear of the car . . . the rear seat, I mean, then got out. The wind was tearing across the moor, the rain was coming down like stair rods, I could feel the weight of it on my shoulders. Lovely. I mean, no one was moving on a night like that. Took her out of the car, took the letter opener from her body and put it on the pile of clothing. Didn't want to get blood on the interior of the car, it was a demonstration vehicle, you see, Dr Simnal, and it could be traced to me. Anyway, I took her body from the car, she wasn't a big lass, she was as light as a feather, no weight at all, and I took her up to the drystone wall and dropped her out of sight on the other side, got back in the car and found my way home. It was remote, the high Pennines, but every road leads somewhere and eventually I found a "B" road, and that led to an "A" road, and I picked up the signs for Keighley, and then from there I got to Leeds and then I was on the road to Selby and home. She wasn't found for three days, and then only by chance, the weather you understand, folks didn't wander far from shelter, but a forestry worker saw her from a distance from the cab of his four-by-four. He couldn't tell what it was at first, but he thought it didn't look right, so he investigated.'

'What did you do with the clothing?'

'And the handbag . . . don't forget the handbag and the

letter opener. The clothing, there wasn't much of it, weather like that but she was hardly wearing anything at all, all for the sake of fashion. Women . . . you can't fathom them. But I folded up all her clothing and put it in a weighted bin liner with a hole in the top, so the air would escape and the thing would sink. I dropped that into the River Wharfe at Selby, black, black water and lots of lovely mud at the bottom. It was well weighted, three house bricks, it's probably worked its way into the mud by now. Won't be easy to recover it, but I'll take the police to the spot where I threw it in. I could do with a day out. You know I don't get to breathe fresh air.'

Maurice Simnal didn't reply but he thought, 'poor you'.

'The shoes, the empty handbag, and the cheap watch she wore, I left in the doorway of charity shops in York. You know how folk leave donations in the doorways of charity shops when the shop is closed?'

'Yes.'

'Well, it was about seven in the evening, I found a charity shop, left the shoes on top of a pile of donations that were already there; the watch I pushed through the letterbox of another charity shop, and the handbag I left in the doorway of a third charity shop, also on top of a pile of donations.'

'And the contents of the handbag?'

'Oh, tipped them into the Wharfe as well, purse, lipstick, all the other bits and pieces that women find to fill these handbags, all heavier than water, all sank instantly. Had the car cleaned and valeted. Sold it the following week. The letter opener, that went back into my father's bureau.'

'The police will want to recover that, it's a murder weapon.'

'Doubtless they will. I am sure my good father will be happy to surrender it. He's very public-spirited. But you've met him, of course.' Sweet reclined and clasped his hands behind his head. 'So now the West Yorkshire police will be calling on me. I do love this attention. I'm somebody now, I have a name . . . in here I mean.'

'So you said.'

'But that's it.' Sweet stood.

'It is?

'Yes, that's it for today. I murdered her because she was there. That's it. I'm not talking about any other part of my life, not today anyway. Maybe in time. But for now you'll have to keep interviewing the others in here, I hear they are quite co-operative.'

'Some are,' Simnal nodded. 'Some are.'

When Sweet had walked back to the ward, clearly terminating the interview on his terms, Simnal stood, but also in his own time, on his own terms and went to the nursing station where David was on duty. 'Do you still think he's sane?'

'Oh yes,' David raised his eyebrows, 'but then I am only a psychiatric nurse, I'm not degreed-up. But more and more, day by day, I am certain of his sanity. I haven't seen anything at all to suggest otherwise. He's wangled himself a soft bed in a hospital because we, you, all the professionals involved, are confusing evil with insanity. But the two are not the same.'

'You're a cynic, David.'

'Me?' David smiled. 'Possibly. We all get cynical if we stay in the same job long enough. Maybe I am ready to move on. But, but, but . . .' he pointed a pen towards Humphrey Sweet, by then sitting in front of the television, 'but he sticks out here, sticks out like a sore thumb. The other nurses feel the same. He sticks out because he is the only one who isn't insane. But that's just my . . . our . . . tuppence worth.'

On the pathway leading from the DSPD, Simnal met Ruth Day, who was walking towards him. He stopped as he saw her, involuntarily, then walked on. She halted and waited for him to reach her. They stood facing each other, looking into each other's eyes, but not as before. This time he felt there was anger in his eyes and, he thought, a touch of sorrow in hers.

'My husband told me he met you at the opening of the new clinic at the Princess Alice.'

'He did.'

After a pause, Ruth said, 'I don't know what to say. I mean, he more or less told me the content of the conversation.'

'There's nothing you can say.' Simnal allowed a note of anger to creep into his voice.

'I thought if I had had your sympathy . . . man the rescuer.'

Simnal groaned and looked skyward. His eye caught by a high-flying bird and he followed it for a second or two. He then looked at Ruth Day. 'I would rather have had the truth from the outset.' He paused. 'I also have to say that I am a little . . . no, a lot, disappointed that you, as a psychologist, a student of human nature, should hope to have a relationship based on a game and on lies.'

'So it's over?'

'It has to be. Sorry, but it has to be.' He turned from her and walked away.

'What about Humphrey Sweet?' she called after him. 'What about him?'

'Well, what about him?'

'We are co-working this case.'

'Not any more. We'll both still see him, but not as a team. We'll work independently of each other. I'm about finished with him, anyway. He's not being very co-operative with respect to my area of research.'

'Reluctant to talk about his early years?'

'Yes.' Simnal detected a wish in Ruth to keep the conversation going, an attempt to salvage something. 'I can get sufficient material from other patients, so I don't need him, but I'm happy to see him while he's confessing to his crimes, in order to help the police.'

'Seems you are the only one he'll speak to.'

'Yes.' He turned and walked briskly away.

There followed another long and empty-feeling weekend for Maurice Simnal. His house seemed too large, as did his bed. He couldn't settle to anything during the day, rather he tended to 'nibble' at jobs, the garden, the endless house-work. In the evening he sat in his chair and by repeatedly pressing the buttons on the remote control he 'channel hopped' the television until, desperate for human company, he strolled across the green as dusk drew in and spent the remainder of the evening in the White Horse. He did that on the busy Friday and Saturday evenings and also on quiet Sunday evening, not at all self-conscious about being a barfly, the only one, alone at the bar. Nonetheless, he was gratified to wake up on the Monday, gratified to have a job to do, so as to occupy his mind. He signed in at St Leonard's Place, checked his pigeonhole, and then signed out to 'the police' giving eleven a.m. as his estimated time of return. He strolled to the police station. It was still just nine-thirty a.m. but the city was bustling and the pavements were begin-ning to bake. Sitting in front of Tom Mautby's desk, enjoying a refreshing mug of tea, he listened as Mautby described his weekend.

'Well, you did for the West Yorkshire police what you did for the Somerset and Avon boys last week. So, thanks for that phone call . . . they interviewed Sweet over the weekend. He was, by all accounts, quite co-operative. No remorse, they said.'

'No, that's conspicuous by its absence.' Simnal sipped the tea. 'As is insight into the distress he has caused. He's a very self-orientated personality, the sun shines just for him, he believes.'

'As with all murderers . . .' Mautby wiped his brow. 'I've been doing this job a long time, turned a corner recently, and now I can see my retirement on the horizon, and it's not a bad sight at all, but I tell you, Maurice, I have never arrested a murderer who did not think the same as Sweet, as you say, "the sun shines just for me" attitude.'

'So I have heard.'

'It's frightening.'

'Very. It would be impossible to live with someone who had that attitude.'

'Unfortunately, many people do. We see them on Saturday nights, victims of domestic violence . . . men as well as women. I tell you, there's a lot of battered husbands out there.'

'So I believe.'

'It's easy for a woman to walk into a police station and report her husband for assaulting her, but for a man to walk into a police station to report his wife for beating him up . . . that's next to impossible. Battered husbands suffer in silence. Anyway . . . Geraldine Toovey . . . nineteen when she flagged down a taxi which was anything but a taxi.'

'Nineteen,' Simnal sighed. 'All murders are tragic . . . but when the victim is so young . . . when life is ahead of them.'

'Yes. I think we all feel the same way. She was a hairdresser and had just fallen out with her boyfriend.'

Simnal nodded. 'Sweet said she seemed to be walking angrily. Like that lad in Bristol, just the wrong place at the wrong time, and he wouldn't have stopped if she hadn't flagged him down. He has indicated he has more to tell me, so we'll see what he tells me next session.'

'Still seeing him on a weekly basis?'

'Yes. There's no time pressure, sadly . . . and I don't think he'll tell me any sooner, anyway. We're playing his game here, and he knows it. He's calling the shots. Any pressure on him and he'll . . .' Simnal drew his fingers across his lips in a sealing motion.

'Well, I'll leave that to you and your expertise.' Tom Mautby stirred his mug of tea with his ballpoint pen. 'I did some digging about Mrs Hood over the weekend. I was able to access the archives of High Royds, now sadly closed. It was, still is, a lovely building. The archives have been relocated to central Leeds.'

Simnal listened.

'She's a lady with a history.'

'Oh?'

'Yes, and a cloud of suspicion is beginning to gather above milady's head.'

'Again . . . oh?'

'She has a history of psychiatric ill health. She has been hospitalized a few times and is presently on medication.'

'I did wonder. She had a lacklustre flatness of affect that is so common amongst the mentally ill, but it's not unique to mental ill health, some perfectly sane people just don't have any spark about them. I thought she was sane because her house and garden are very well ordered, not the confused household and rambling overgrown garden I would normally associate with psychiatric ill health. I thought it very likely she had contract gardeners to do her garden, but even having an interest in its appearance is a sign of good health. So I just assumed that she had a flat personality. I think Ruth Day did so too, she didn't comment otherwise.'

'I see. Well, the police at Castleford are taking a renewed interest in the disappearance of her husband.'

'So he didn't go back to live with his family at Castleford?'

'No. He remains a missing person. Myself and a Castleford cop, one Jimmy Dancer . . .'

'Lovely name.' Simnal smiled.

'Does have a certain ring to it, doesn't it? Well, he and I visited Mr Hood's brother . . .' Mautby went on to relate the details of his joint visit with Dancer to Ralph Hood's home. When he had concluded, he asked, 'Would someone who is psychiatrically ill be more or less likely to be open to manipulation?'

154

'Oh . . .' Simnal reclined in the chair, 'that's a big one. Off the top of my head I'd say it was unanswerable. I can think of some psychiatrically ill people who could not be manipulated, so certain are they of their own correctness in all things. Equally, I can think of one or two psychiatrically ill people who are so battered by their illness that their will has gone and they offer instant and unquestioning obedience . . . some do, some don't. Just like sane people . . . some do, some don't.'

'Kathleen Hood?'

'Yes. She's more than a hospital visitor; she wasn't wholly truthful with myself and Dr Day. We didn't believe her when she told us Humphrey Sweet had not mentioned his alter egos called "Lenny" and "Alf". We had the impression that Sweet is using her, but for what, we don't know. All we could do was to warn her.'

'Well, it is for that reason that the police at Castleford are taking a renewed interest in the disappearance of Edward Hood. She was visiting Sweet before her husband disappeared.'

'That is interesting.' Simnal spoke, slowly, softly. 'Very interesting.'

'Ah . . . forgot to tell you.' Mautby smiled. 'Yes, there was a flower.'

'On Geraldine Toovey's body?'

'Not quite on the body, but resting atop the drystone wall a little further along from the point where he left her body. Once again it was caught by chance on the police photographs. They didn't connect it to the murder at the time but fortunately one wide-angled shot of the scene captured it by chance. His work all right.'

Simnal strolled back to his office at St Leonard's. York had become noticeably busier, with open-topped buses and horse-drawn carriages competing for road space with everyday traffic. The sun beat down, the pavement radiated heat. He was very pleased to step into his air-conditioned workplace. He signed in, and after exchanging pleasantries with the receptionist, he checked his pigeonhole. 'David from Kempton DSPD asks if you could call at your earliest convenience.' Simnal walked to his office and sat at his desk and hung his jacket over the back of his chair. He picked up the phone, dialled nine for an outside line and then the Kempton Hospital number. When his call was answered, he asked to be put through to the DSPD nursing station.

'DSPD, Nurse Kehoe speaking.'

'David?' Simnal asked, thinking he recognized the voice.

'Yes. Is that Dr Simnal?'

'Yes it is. I've just returned, picked up your message. You asked me to phone you?'

'Yes, it's Humphrey Sweet, he's on a real high.'

'He is?'

'He was visited by the police over the weekend.'

'So I have heard.' Simnal pressed the phone to his ear with his shoulder as he rolled up his shirtsleeves.

'Well, he enjoyed the attention and he wants more. He's the King of the Hill now. He wants to consolidate. He asked me to ask you to visit him. He's got another tale. He's bursting to tell you something.'

'Well, I could come over this afternoon but I don't want him to think I am at his beck and call. Let's see . . .' Simnal consulted his diary. 'I'll come on Wednesday morning, direct from my house, say about nine thirty?'

'Thank you. It will do him no harm to wait.'

Simnal breakfasted that Wednesday morning as rain fell. The rainfall was short, very intensive, very welcome and very refreshing. It had stopped by the time he left his house and he enjoyed the rural smell of soil and shrubs, which had been heightened by the sudden shower. He also enjoyed the sight of the near-perfect rainbow which hung over

Hutton Cranswick, and the air so clean now. It was, he thought, too pleasant a morning to be spent inside the locked ward at Kempton Hospital, and it was with no little reluctance that he drove there.

Simnal had delayed for forty-eight hours before visiting Sweet, so as to make the point he wanted to make; nonetheless, despite the delay he found Humphrey Sweet to be as David Kehoe had described: 'on a real high'.

'Sorry you couldn't come earlier, Maurice . . . sorry, Dr Simnal.' Sweet smiled, his bottomless eyes seemed to Simnal to be penetrating his mind, as if reading his thoughts and that look, it was there again, the eye contact, the smile, sucking him in, pulling him closer.

'David tells me you want to talk to me, another tale to tell. Is that the case?'

'Yes. I've made it, I'm top dog here now. I get proper respect.'

'I am pleased for you.'

'Yes. Well, I'm here for a long time so I want to keep my place. Here you get respect for things you'd get attacked in the showers for in prison. It's just how it is.'

'So I believe.'

'I wouldn't survive in prison, Dr Simnal, but here I am given my due.'

'So what do you want to tell me?'

'Another female. Sort of balances things, don't you think?'

Simnal didn't reply. He waited for Sweet to continue. The only thing that Sweet continued to do was give Simnal approving eye contact. Eventually Simnal conceded and said, 'Go on.'

'Middle-aged dame walking her little dog. No one about, banged her over the head, left the dog tied to a tree, carried her body a bit away, hid it in a ditch. Not been found yet. That was a year or two ago now. Don't know her name. Didn't go through her shoulder bag. I covered the body up

157

and made myself scarce. Never heard a mention of her on the news or in the press.'

'Where was this?'

'Lincolnshire. Went a little bit south, not as far as Bristol but went south of the Humber. Who would link a middle-aged woman who was murdered by being banged over the head and left clothed, with a young female who was stabbed and left naked . . . with a snapped neck, and when one is in the Pennines and the other is in Lincolnshire?'

'Few, if any,' Simnal spoke softly, 'but as you have said, the only drawback is that you never get any credit . . . never know infamy in your lifetime.'

'Strangely enough, I wanted to stop doing it. A bit of me wanted to be caught and that bit of me grew each day.' Simnal thought Sweet's comment interesting. In it, Simnal saw a glimmer of remorse, a glimmer of insight. In fact, he saw a glimmer of sanity. Sweet might not have escaped showers in prison after all. He asked, 'So where in Lincolnshire did you bury her? Which part and parcel?'

Sweet smiled. 'In the parcel of Kesteven, there's a little village called Hillside, which is rich, because the landscape round there is pretty flat. To the south of the village there is a wood. Tell the police to release their sniffer dogs in the wood. They'll find her very quickly.'

'Hillside,' Simnal said.

'In Kesteven, parcel of Lincolnshire.' Sweet smiled.

Maurice Simnal's jaw sagged as he absorbed the implications of what Tom Mautby told him.

'It's the only explanation.' Mautby's countenance was grave, serious, solemn. 'He had to have had help.'

Simnal had instantly reported the content of the conversation he had had with Humphrey Sweet to Mautby, who relayed all information to the Lincolnshire police. The following Friday, shortly after Simnal had arrived at his office, his phone had rung. It was Mautby who had said, 'I think we should chat.'

'The Lincolnshire police came back to me late yesterday.' Mautby had patted the phone on his desk after the preliminaries, and after a perspiring Simnal had taken a seat in front of Mautby's desk. 'They found the body exactly where Sweet had told you it would be. In a small wood near a village called Hillside. It was under a tree.'

'A tree!' Simnal gasped. 'Sweet told me he had covered it with foliage. I thought a few branches, some shrubs . . .'

'No.' It was then that Mautby's countenance became grave. 'A tree, a large tree, it had been uprooted some years before in a gale . . . that storm, remember? She was under it.'

'How big was the tree?' Simnal asked. 'I mean there are trees and there are trees.'

'This tree took four constables to lift. That sort of tree.' And as Simnal gaped, Mautby concluded: 'It's the only explanation. He had to have help.'

The two men sat in silence. Simnal broke it by saying 'Alf and Lenny?'

'Yes,' Mautby nodded, 'that's what I thought.'

Simnal put his hand up to his mouth. He then removed it. 'This might mean that he doesn't suffer from MPD.'

'Exactly. When I was a young copper an old copper said to me, "Let 'em run off at the mouth, they'll talk themselves into the dock."'

'That's Humphrey Sweet.' Simnal glanced out of the window of Tom Mautby's office. 'He can't stop boasting. So confident he's in control that he'd put his neck into the noose just for the fun of it, completely certain nothing could happen to anyone as clever as him. So much for our assessment and diagnosis skills.'

'Well . . .' Mautby smiled. 'You might still be right. He might have, what was it . . .?'

'Multiple Personality Disorder.'

'Yes, he might still have it. He might be barking mad, and still have had help with this murder. Those two names, "Alf" and "Lenny", might still be inside his head somewhere. But this case has blown wide open for the Lincolnshire boys. What was a missing person file is now a murder inquiry. They've got a top team on it. She was a local worthy and the press were all over her disappearance. They request your assistance.'

'They've got it. Anything I can do to be of help.'

Mautby smiled. 'Good. They're travelling up today, going direct to Kempton. They'd like you to sit in on the interview.'

'With pleasure. When are they due to arrive?'

Mautby glanced at his watch. 'Well, with a favourable following wind, and if they catch the right tide at the Humber, I'd say in about thirty minutes.'

Simnal grinned and stood. 'Do me a favour, please?'

'If I can.'

'Phone Kempton, DSPD Unit, ask them to wait for me; I'll be there in about . . . well, less than an hour. Once I leave York it's a clear road.'

Humphrey Sweet relaxed. He wore a scarlet tee shirt, blue jeans, jogging shoes. He smiled. He was clean-shaven, hair groomed, teeth flashed white, only his impenetrable bottomless blue eyes indicated a dark side to his psyche. Were it not for those eyes, Simnal thought, were it not for those eyes, he might be auditioning for the lead male part in a feature film.

'You know me, Humphrey,' Simnal said. 'This is Detective Sergeant Parsloe of the Lincolnshire police.'

Parsloe, a heavy-set man with a silver handlebar moustache, grunted and nodded at Sweet, who smiled in return.

'And this is Detective Sergeant Winter, also of the Lincolnshire Constabulary.'

160

Winter, younger, more athletic than Parsloe, nodded but remained silent.

'And also a detective sergeant,' Sweet observed. 'Two DS's for little me. I am honoured.'

'So,' Parsloe spoke in a slow Lincolnshire drawl. It was a regional accent with which Simnal was unfamiliar. 'Are you going to help us or not?'

'Why not?' Sweet settled back in his chair. 'I helped the Bristol and Avon police, I helped the West Yorkshire police, and the Lancashire police. I'm a . . . what is the term, Maurice?'

'A variable serial killer.' Simnal let a note of disapproval enter his voice. He knew that it would interrupt the interview if he corrected Sweet in respect of form of address and he knew that Sweet knew it.

'That's it . . . a "variable serial killer". Maurice is writing an article about me, to be published in learned journals, aren't you, Maurice? It will do us both good. He will become established as a forensic pathologist and the world will know about me. Do you gentlemen from Lincolnshire know what a variable serial killer is?'

'Yes,' Parsloe growled.

'Dr Simnal told us before we came to the ward,' Winter added, with equal ice in his voice.

'I am the first. Well . . . the first to be identified, aren't I, Maurice?'

Simnal didn't reply.

'So, are you going to help us?' Parsloe asked again.

'Why not?' Sweet shrugged.

'Tell us what happened.'

'I told Maurice.'

'Tell us.'

'Knocked her on the head, tied up her dog, left her in a wood covered with branches.'

'Not exactly,' Parsloe replied. He was clearly the senior DS, so Simnal noted, but he also noticed how DS Winter was in close support, eyeing Sweet with a piercing gimlet stare.

'In the first place the dog was dogs – two Alsatians. Not just Alsatians but retired police dogs. Probably too old for police work but plenty of life in them . . . and I wouldn't mess with one, let alone two. And they were left tied to a tree. They were tied with a length of rope that seemed to have been previously obtained for the sole purpose of restraining the dogs. When they were found, they were well tangled up in it and in a state of distress.'

'It would be very distressing for police-trained Alsatians not to be able to do anything to protect their owner,' Winter added. 'They had to be put down.'

'The distress never left them, you see,' Parsloe explained. 'Too agitated to be re-homed.'

'So there's two more victims for you.'

Sweet smiled. 'Animals don't count, do they, Maurice? Maurice will tell you what I did with a cat and a rabbit and a goldfish, won't you, Maurice?'

Simnal remained silent.

'The victim, Mrs Baverstock by name, was found two miles from where she was abducted, in broad daylight.'

'Yes, it was a particularly fine day. I recall it quite well.'

'Under branches?'

'Sorry?'

'You said you left her under branches.'

'Yes, I did.'

'Which in a sense you did,' Parsloe conceded. 'If only because branches were attached to the tree trunk you lifted on top of her in a natural hollow in Swine's Wood.'

'Where?'

'It's the name of the wood near Hillside.'

'Ah.'

'You placed her in a natural hollow on the floor of the wood and lifted a fallen tree trunk and overlaid it on her body. Then concealed her from view with branches. She wasn't found earlier because the wood is swampy, quite boggy in places, and so those with local knowledge avoid it. Dog walkers, courting couples and children prefer neighbouring woods. Foxes don't mind, though; her body had been ravaged by scavengers and predators.'

'She was identified by her rings, her handbag . . . DNA clinched it.'

'That was quick!' Sweet inclined his head.

'We are quick when we need to be,' Winter said acidly.

'So . . . look at this from our point of view, Humphrey. Broad daylight, a rope brought with the purpose of restraining. Alsatians, carried for two miles, probably in the back of a motor vehicle, not robbed, and clumsily concealed in a wood where few people venture . . . the only thing we are satisfied with is your explanation of banging her on the head. Her skull was like a piece of crazy paving.' Parsloe paused. 'You see, Humphrey, this speaks loudly and clearly to myself and DS Winter here, and other officers in this investigation, of premeditation. It speaks of motive for wanting to kill Mrs Baverstock for reasons other than the thrill.'

'Otherwise you would have robbed her. She was carrying over one hundred pounds in her purse. You didn't even open her handbag,' Winter added.

'And most importantly, Humphrey, most importantly, it speaks of at least two, possibly three accomplices.'

'Rather makes it a bit different from all your other murders, all your other victims,' Winter scowled. 'It means this one has a story behind it.'

Simnal inclined his body forward and turned to the police officers. This was a police interview, protocol had to be observed. 'If I may, gentlemen?'

'Please . . .' Parsloe extended an open palm.

Simnal addressed Sweet. 'If you don't co-operate, Humphrey, that implies guilt. By guilt, I mean an awareness of guilt and an insight into your actions. That in turn implies sanity.'

Peter Turnbull

Humphrey Sweet's face drained of blood. His jaw dropped. He stood and tapped on the glass partition. David Kehoe, again the nurse on duty, stood in response to the tap on the pane of glass. 'I want to go back to the ward,' Sweet stammered. 'I'm going back to the ward.'

When Parsloe and Winter and Simnal were alone in the room, Parsloe turned to Simnal and asked, 'Would you care to help us further?'

'Any way I can.'

'You seem to have a finger on the pulse of our boy . . .'

Simnal raised his eyebrows. 'Well, I thought I had. Now I am not sure.'

'More than us as least. We'd like you to be part of our team, not as a police officer, of course.'

'Understood.'

'But as brains to pick.'

'You could do that by phone.'

'We need you to be more hands-on,' Winter explained. 'We talked about this on the way up here. We have to link him,' he pointed to Sweet who by then was nearing the far end of the ward, 'to this murder by more than his confession. And we need to find his accomplices.'

'And you know the sort of questions to ask.'

'I think I can make arrangements,' Simnal smiled. 'Yes, I am sure I can.'

Eight

Simnal had enjoyed a pleasant weekend with Toby. The new rendezvous point he had suggested was the concourse at York Railway Station. It had been tried and proved eminently more practical than crowded Lendal Bridge. Interestingly, he thought, the rendezvous was in some ways harder. He found himself looking forward, not to just to seeing Toby again, but Jane as well. When they met, Jane had smiled at him. It was a brief smile, but it was there. They talked longer than was usual at such times and he felt that their parting was harder than usual. He and Toby remained in York that morning and afternoon. They visited the National Railway Museum again, at Toby's insistence, although Simnal did not object – there was in him a small boy's fascination with steam locomotives which he knew would never leave him, and he was indeed happy to take with him to his grave. They ate together at an Italian restaurant and joined the 'Ghost Walk' round the medieval city enjoying the humour of their guide who was, thought Simnal, once again splendidly, strikingly, dressed in Victorian costume. They drove home to Hutton Cranswick as dusk fell, shared a little supper and a tired Toby was soon abed and asleep. Simnal remained awake a little longer, watching a chat show on TV, and then he too retired for the night. Sunday was spent quietly, feeding the ducks on the duck pond after breakfast, where Simnal, once again, felt that half a family wasn't a viable unit. He felt intuitively, and knew professionally, that a child needs both parents, and he felt the guilt deeply, that were it not for his indiscretion, then Toby, his issue, his responsibility, would still be enjoying the company and presence of both parents. On Sunday evening they had journeyed to York to 'hand over' Toby to his mother. Again, there was an unusual but real warmth in the meeting of estranged husband and wife, and again, there was an unusual but real reluctance to part.

On the Monday, having made arrangements and obtained approval from the Home Office, Simnal, with a bag packed for one week, drove to Lincoln. He drove directly to the Parcels Hotel where a room had been reserved for him by the Lincolnshire constabulary, booked in, and walked out of the hotel to 'take in the city', never having been before. He found himself impressed by the grandeur of the cathedral and intrigued by the narrow streets. It was, he observed, very similar to York in many ways. He lunched, satisfyingly, in a pub called the Brown Bear, and then walked to the police station, where he was cordially met by Parsloe and Winter. The former suggested that they drive out to see the 'relic' of the deceased.

'The what?' Simnal asked.

'The relic,' Parsloe had said. 'Car park's this way.' He indicated the rear of the building.

'He belongs to an earlier era,' Winter explained. 'It's just his way. "Parsloe the ancient", that's what he's called in this nick. He likes old words, don't you, Jimmy?' Winter's mirthful voice echoed in the gleamingly clean, blue-hued, sanitized corridor.

'Love 'em,' Jimmy Parsloe replied. 'Love 'em. I should have been a wordsmith.'

'"Relic" is the latest fad,' Winter said. 'It'll be with us for a few weeks and then it'll be replaced by something else. Found it in a graveyard, didn't you, Jim?' Winter held open a door for Parsloe and Simnal.

'Yep . . . love reading graves.' Parsloe grinned. 'It's kind of a hobby. If I have an hour or so to pass in a strange town, I go and find a cemetery and read the gravestones. Fascinating. Found a gravestone of a man "and also his relic". Dated about 1820 it was. Made inquiries . . .'

'As a policeman would,' added Winter.

'Found out that "relic" was the surviving spouse of a marriage, usually, but not always, the wife. Later in the century the term "widow" and "widower" were used.'

'Ah, I see,' Simnal said. 'So, we're off to see the widower, the "relic" of Mrs Baverstock?'

'Got it in one,' Winter laughed.

The 'relic' of Mrs Baverstock lived in a rambling, late Victorian house on the southern outskirts of Lincoln. The garden seemed to Simnal to be badly overgrown, the paint on the house was peeling. A Morris Traveller stood in the drive with all four wheels deflated, and the varnish on the ash frame, like the paint on the house, had peeled badly in the east of England sun. It was, thought Simnal, the property and possessions of a man who had 'given up', who had lost the will to live.

Parsloe announced their presence with a solid, authoritative tap, tap . . . tap on the metal doorknocker. The door was opened after a short pause by a white-haired man with bifocal spectacles, wearing a yellow waistcoat over a check shirt, above cavalry twill trousers. His feet were encased in comfortable-looking sandals and woollen socks. He smiled a gap-toothed smile. 'Police? I got your phone call . . .'

'Yes, sir.' Parsloe flashed his ID. 'DS Parsloe, DS Winter and this gentleman is Dr Simnal, a Home Office psychologist, who's assisting us.'

'Come in, do.' Mr Baverstock stood to one side.

Once seated in the neat and cleanly kept living room, Parsloe asked Mr Baverstock if he knew of anyone who would want to harm his late wife.

'Well, I've thought. The police asked me that all those months ago when Gwen was murdered.' Henry Baverstock

167

glanced out of the window of his living room into the untidy rear garden. 'Let the garden go since Gwen passed. Have a lady to come and see to my house – Czech by birth. Nice girl. Came and did the house then went. Came and did the house and cooked me a meal, but ate separately. Came and did the house and cooked a meal and brought her daughter who enjoys crashing through the bushes and generally exploring the garden, but still ate separately. Then one day there were three places set for the midday meal.' He turned to look at his visitors. 'Methinks milady has designs on an old widower who has no heirs and is worth a lot of money – by Czech standards anyway. Anyway, I still can't think of anyone who'd want to murder her. She had a temper. Her tongue had quite an edge to it, but you kept on her good side . . . if you knew how, and I had the best part of forty years to get that right.' He sighed. 'Why the renewed interest?'

'Well,' Parsloe sat forward, 'a man has confessed to her murder.'

'Oh!' Henry Baverstock's mouth opened. 'Do you mean to say I shall live to see justice done, after all?'

'Probably. Much depends on what we can find out about Mrs Baverstock in the days and weeks prior to her murder. Perhaps, Dr Simnal, you might explain?'

Simnal leaned forward, resting his elbows on his knees. 'Well, it's a long story, sir,' he said, 'and doubtless you'll be hearing and reading about it in the media, but the gist is that a . . . gentleman came to our attention, confessing to a string of murders . . .'

'Gentleman?' Henry Baverstock smiled a civil and, Simnal thought, a learned smile. 'I like your diplomacy, young man.' Simnal nodded in appreciation of the compliment. He also smiled inwardly: it had been a long time since he had been addressed as 'young man'. He realized it was certainly the last time he would be thus addressed and he then knew a certain sadness. 'Well, this said gentleman is believed to be mentally ill. I emphasize believed. His assessment in that respect is still incomplete. Either he is or he isn't. To put it simply, we have yet to agree on a diagnosis.'

'If he's not mad he's bad,' Baverstock offered, 'and if he's not bad, then he's mad.'

'In a nutshell, yes. But he's in a secure facility. Whatever he has done in the past, he won't harm another member of the public again. Nursing staff and patients might be at risk, but he won't prowl the streets again. Ever.'

'That's reassuring,' Baverstock smiled. 'Confess I have mixed feelings about Gwen being murdered by a serial killer. On the one hand, I am relieved that she did not antagonize anybody to the extent that they murdered her, but on the other is the sense of needlessness, of waste, of futility, of being in the wrong place at the wrong time. If she had visited her sister, as planned, she would be alive now. Probably.'

'She was visiting her sister when she was murdered?' Parsloe asked.

'Yes. She intended to visit the day earlier but had to delay the visit. Her sister lives about three quarters of an hour's drive from here. She drove down to Hillside, which is on land that is as flat as a billiard table, hence the name,' Baverstock chuckled. 'Where Gwen grew up, and where her sister still lives. She doesn't like keeping the dogs cooped up in the car and then in her sister's cottage, they got fractious quickly. Alsatians, you see, they need an awful lot of exercise, so it was Gwen's habit that after the visit she would exercise the dogs before doing the return journey. It was while exercising the dogs that she must have been abducted. In broad daylight and taken from two Alsatians . . . ex-police Alsatians at that.'

'So we believe,' Parsloe said.

'You see, Mr Baverstock,' Simnal spoke. 'This is why we are particularly interested in your wife's murder. We are sure that Sweet did it.'

'Sweet?'

'The name of the man I mentioned. Humphrey Sweet, by name.'

'Sweet.' Baverstock smiled. 'What an ironic name for a multiple murderer. Humphrey Sweet . . . sounds so innocuous, so homely. It sounds like the name of a toy shop proprietor, or a corner newsagent. Well, a rose by any other name . . . as is said. Sorry, I interject . . .'

'No worries.' Simnal smiled. He found himself liking Henry Baverstock. 'The issue with the murder of Mrs Baverstock is that it seems to stand out amongst the other murders Sweet committed, in that there is an indication that Mrs Baverstock was targeted, specifically so. I mean, specifically her.'

'Oh?'

'Yes, the rope used to restrain the dogs. It seems to have been brought along for the purpose.'

'I see.'

'And you have just told us that she was following a settled routine. After visiting her sister, she would exercise the dogs . . . it suggests somebody knew where she'd be, and when she'd be there.'

'So, she wasn't necessarily in the wrong place at the wrong time?'

'Perhaps not, sir.'

'Well, she didn't have many friends but I can't think of anyone who'd want to murder her. Heavens, no . . .'

'The other thing is that there is clear evidence of other people being involved. One man alone couldn't have abducted your wife in broad daylight, and restrained two Alsatians, and driven her away to where she was found.'

'No . . .' Baverstock spoke softly, 'one person couldn't do that.'

'And your wife's body was found under a tree.'

'In a hollow, covered by an old tree trunk, yes. So I was

told. I visited the spot to lay flowers . . . but by then the tree trunk had been moved back, of course.'

'It apparently took four constables to lift it off her body.'

'So, you're saying that it would take the same effort to lift it on to her body?'

'Yes,' Simnal nodded. 'There is a clear conspiracy here. And to return to the dogs . . . it's likely the murderers were known to Mrs Baverstock, and her dogs. Otherwise they couldn't have got near her.'

'Yes, the dogs were very protective of her. I didn't worry about her going out alone, so long as the dogs were with her. Shows how wrong you can be.'

'So . . . in furtherance of the issue of accomplices, do you know of any person called "Lenny" or "Alf"?'

'Lenny, Alf? Can't say I do. That would be Leonard and Alfred, I assume?'

'We assume so,' Simnal said, 'but we know them only as Lenny and Alf.'

'Not many Alfs about . . . not these days. I like the name, I confess. Quite a few Leonards, but not Alfreds . . . not a common name these days. But either way, I know no Lenny or Alfred on a personal level that is within our circle of friends and family. In fact the only Lenny I know is the librarian at the college where I used to teach. I know of no Alfred or Alfie at all. My wife's sister might know of someone of either name.'

'She is?'

'Gertrude Platt. Miss. She never married. She lives at Rose Cottage, Hillside.'

Simnal, from the rear seat of the car, as he and Parsloe and Winter drove away from Henry Baverstock's house, said, 'Interesting.'

'What is?' Parsloe slowed the car as he approached a major road.

'His attitude. There was a sort of joy about him, about

171

Mr Baverstock. He wasn't the grief-stricken . . . relic . . . that I was expecting.'

'Wasn't, was he?' Winter added. Then he added '"Relic",' and smiled.

'He admitted his wife had a difficult personality . . . a temper . . . a tongue with an edge . . . what else did he say? Oh yes, if you kept on the right side of her. Blimey . . . I have the impression that poor Mr Baverstock was the cuckolded, henpecked, downtrodden husband of a foul-tempered shrew of a woman and now he has a peaceful house at long last. No wonder he seemed happy and content with life. Just fighting off the Czech predator now. No photographs of Mrs B. either. Interesting.'

'We'll probably be able to gauge the past from the present,' Parsloe said as he overtook a slow-moving lorry. 'We'll see what Miss Platt is like. More importantly, see if she knows anybody called Lenny or Alfie.'

Rose Cottage, Hillside, revealed itself to be a small, white-washed cottage with yellow roses growing in varnished wooden tubs either side of the yellow front door. The door was opened rapidly and aggressively upon Winter's knock by a short, pinched-faced woman in her sixties who looked up at Winter and snapped, 'What!'

Simnal thought that much was explained, if Mrs Baverstock was like her surviving sister. Little wonder Mr Baverstock seemed to be relishing the tranquillity of his house, he thought, and was happy to let the garden run wild. The poor man had probably been nagged about the lawn and the herbaceous border until he was at his wits' end.

'Police.' Winter showed his ID.

'Well! What?' Miss Platt spat the words. She was, guessed Simnal, not much more than four and a half feet tall, but wasn't at all intimidated by three men at her cottage door, two of whom were very large police officers.

'It's about your sister.'

'Gwen?'

'Yes.'

'She was murdered.'

Simnal could detect no softening in the woman's manner, even upon the mention of her late sister.

'Yes. We'd like to talk to you about that. May we come in?'

'If you must.'

The interior of Rose Cottage was neatly kept, brushed and wiped clean, and smelled of furniture polish and air freshener. The rear door had been left open to allow the small house to ventilate in the heat. Flies were kept out by a veil of plastic ribbons hanging from the top of the door-frame.

'What then?' Miss Platt stood in the middle of the floor of her small living room, standing up to Simnal and the two police officers like, Simnal thought, a Jack Russell standing up to three Dobermans. 'What now?'

'We'd like to talk about the murder of your sister,' Parsloe said calmly.

'I assumed that!'

'Do the names "Alf" and "Lenny" or "Alfred" and "Leonard" mean anything to you? Do you know of anybody of those names in any capacity?'

'Yes, I do.'

The stunned silence in the cottage could almost be felt.

'You do?'

'I said so. Yes, I do.'

'Who are they?'

'They belong to the Foxes. That family is bad. Always has been, always will be.'

'The Foxes?'

'Frederick Fox, his wife Maxine, and their children, except the children are all adults now. If anything happens in Hillside, any theft, any damage, it's always the work of the Foxes. Always. They're vermin. Me and my sister led a campaign to have them evicted. Alfred and Leonard belong to them, but they've left home now. Haven't seen them for a while. I hear tell they're living north of the Humber. Which is good for this village. North of the Tyne would be even better.'

'Where can we find them?' Winter asked.

'You can walk from here. Hillside, being Hillside . . . small and compact . . . left out of the door. Right at the Bull Inn, road called "Dutch Elms Lane". House at the end of the lane. The lane's a dead end and the house at the dead end is the pit where the Foxes live.'

'That's interesting, Poppet.' Nora Worth stood at the window of her home, looking out of the net curtains. 'There's goings-on at that house, Poppet. Seen her before a few times but not those two. Those two we haven't seen before, have we, Poppet? But they seem to know their way around. Nothing seems new to them. Been there before, Poppet, we just haven't seen them. Interesting though. Isn't it interesting?'

The directions were perfect, the walk pleasant. The Foxes' house was a rundown-looking cottage with boarded-up windows and old cars and vans in the garden. Chickens roamed, and a grey dog barked once at the arrival of Simnal and the police officers and then gave them no more interest than he paid the chickens. The door of the building was pushed open and a portly, ruddy-faced woman in an apron stood in the doorway. 'What now?' she sighed.

'Police,' said Parsloe.

'You don't have to tell me. The only visitors we get are the police. Haven't seen you before, none of you. Three this time. So now what?'

'I'm not a police officer,' Simnal smiled.

'Well, whatever. We know nothing about it. What's she been saying now?'

'Who?'

'Miss Platt.'

'How did you know we were there?' Parsloe asked.

'You were seen. This is a village. You don't see folk watching you, but strangers . . . they're always watched. And news travels. Tell you the truth, it was our Mark. He was walking home when he saw you go into her cottage. He said the police are talking to Platt. They'll be here soon. And look, here you are'

'You don't like Miss Platt?'

'No. The Platts have lived in this village for generations, churchyard's full of Platts. So have the Foxes. There's always been bad blood between the two families and the Foxes have always been the underdog. Whenever there's a theft, whenever there's vandalism, the police knock on this door. They were here in force when Gwen Platt was murdered, but my boys had an alibi, so did my man. My man was in prison for poaching. Alf and Lenny, well, they were away working. Mark and Tony were still in school then.' A malodorous air seeped from within the Fox house. Simnal and the two officers were relieved that they were clearly not going to be invited inside.

'Where are Alf and Lenny?'

'Why? They're not in any trouble.'

'We just need to confirm their alibi for the murder of Mrs Baverstock.'

'Who?'

'Gwen Platt.'

'Oh . . . aye, she married well, didn't she? She'll always be a Platt so far as we are concerned. You reopening her case, are you? And once again, we're the top of the list of suspects. Give a dog a bad name . . . that's right, isn't it? Once you've stuck a label on a family . . . well, the alibi is the same. They were up in Selby.'

'Where?' Simnal gasped.

'Selby,' Mrs Fox repeated. 'Why, do you know it?'

'Yes,' Simnal nodded. 'Yes, I do.'

175

'Well, that's where they are. Selling posh cars.'

'Selling cars?' Again Simnal gasped.

'Well, not selling . . . not yet, but they clean them, inside and out. Make them right for the customers to buy. Can't remember the name of the garage . . .'

'It's all right,' Simnal said. 'I think I know it.'

Simnal walked the summer evening streets of Lincoln. He had returned to the police station with Parsloe and Winter and informed them of the address of the Cohen dealership in Selby where Humphrey Sweet had been a salesman, and where Alfred and Leonard Fox were most likely to be employed. He had sat in the office with Parsloe, who, glancing at the clock, had said, 'We might just catch 'em,' and who had then phoned the dealership, had indeed 'caught them' and had it confirmed that Leonard and Alfred Fox were indeed employees. 'No . . . nothing to worry about,' Parsloe had said to the manager of the business. 'We'll pay a call tomorrow . . . be obliged if you didn't mention this call. Thanks.' Simnal had then taken his cheery, handshaking leave of Parsloe and Winters and headed back to his hotel room, having decided against returning to Hutton Cranswick. He had, he reasoned, nothing and nobody to go home to. He had an early night and experienced a vivid dream wherein he was bounding across lush, flat countryside, chasing a large white hare. The following morning, after relishing a full English breakfast, he drove directly to Kempton Hospital. He thought himself fortunate not to meet Ruth Day, the embarrassment he would have found acute, and went directly to the DSPD Unit and asked to see Humphrey Sweet. 'No David?' he asked of the nurse whose name badge proclaimed him as 'Stephen'.

'Dave's day off,' Stephen explained genially. 'Even nurses have to rest.'

'I'll say.' Simnal sat in the interview room and waited while Stephen went away to bring Humphrey Sweet to him.

Humphrey Sweet smiled. 'Oh, I'm sorry . . . Dr Simnal.' He slid into the chair opposite Simnal. 'This is a pleasant surprise.'

Simnal remained impassive. 'You'll be getting a visit from the Lincolnshire police.'

'Another visit?'

'Yes, another visit, today or tomorrow . . . probably tomorrow. Today they'll be busy with Alfred and Lenny Fox. Donald and Tiny, I presume?'

Sweet looked startled. Worried.

'You overreached yourself dangling those names in front of us, Humphrey. We found them. It wasn't difficult. Mrs Baverstock had a sister.'

'I didn't know that.' Sweet continued to look uncomfortable.

'Oh, yes. It seems it wasn't so much that Alfred and Leonard helped you, it was more the case that you helped them. They wanted to score a point in a long-running feud between two families.'

'The voices in my head told me that it was all right.'

Simnal smiled inwardly. 'We'll see what Alf and Lenny say to the police. How did you get past the dogs?'

'Lenny had a device, battery powered, handheld, emits a high-pitched sound. Human ear can't detect it, dogs don't like it.'

'Did they run?'

'No. Just lay down while Alf tied the rope to their collars. Tied the rope round a tree. The woman was yelling, screaming, but it didn't bother those two. Once the dogs were tied up, Alf tapped her . . . just once . . . small woman she was . . . she was stunned, like she didn't believe anyone could hit her.

'I brought the van up. Middle of the day but it was quite remote. Bundled her into the back. Lenny gave directions; they were local to the area. Said they knew a wood where no one goes. All the while she was saying, "You

177

can't do this to me" and Alfie says, "Just watch us".'

'Who killed her?'

Humphrey Sweet shrugged. 'Don't know . . . I was driving, those two were in the back. She was alive when they put her in, dead when they pulled her out. All three of us lifted the tree trunk that we put over the body. That was that.'

'How did it come about?'

'The offing of Baverstock? Overheard the two boys in the yard behind the showroom. They were valeting an SEL . . . nice car, and one of them, Alfie, said, "I'd like to kill that old bitch", and Lenny said, "I would too. Always had it in for our family". They didn't know I was there and I came up and said, "I could help you there". I hired a van. They both phoned in sick, I took a day's leave. Went down to Hillside and waited for her. She didn't turn up. We agreed to give it another day. They stayed down there, I returned to Selby. I phoned in sick the next day, it seemed like a flu bug was going round. I drove back down the following day and she turned up, little woman with two huge dogs. Looked a bit silly. Anyway we offed her. The voices in my head said it was all right.'

At seven p.m. that night, Maurice Simnal was physically sick. He vomited violently. Half an hour earlier he had received a phone call from Jane, who, in a quaking voice, gave him the news that every parent dreads.

Toby had been abducted.

He had then asked Jane to come to him, so they could be together. She declined, saying she wanted to stay where she was 'in case there is news', and he didn't suggest he come to her because he knew how cramped was her accommodation. It was an evening of gut-wrenching torture for him. The house, even with its palatial size, became claustrophobic, and he went out for a walk, ensuring that his mobile was switched on. Indeed, he found himself checking his mobile every ten or fifteen minutes to check that it was still switched on. It was when he was walking round the green at Hutton Cranswick, wanting to walk but not wanting to be far from his car, that the realization hit him like a blow to the stomach. There was no evidence, no proof, but the knowledge was as certain as a religious faith. He turned in his steps and ran back to his house, collected his car keys and drove to Kempton Hospital. He walked, with rapid, furious steps to the DSPD Unit, asked a bemused nurse, one 'Roger' by his name badge, to see Humphrey Sweet. When he and Sweet were face to face in the interview room, Simnal demanded, 'No games, Sweet. Where is he?'

'My, Maurice.' Sweet smiled. 'So near my bedtime, too.'

'Where is he?'

'Where's who?'

'Toby. My son.'

'Maurice . . . I've been here. I've never left here.'

'If harm is done . . .' Simnal stepped up to Sweet.

'Sir!' The nurse intervened. 'This is personal. I have to ask you to leave.' He placed his arm between Simnal and Sweet. 'I'll have to call hospital security if you don't leave.'

'You said you'd never had a male child victim. I knew you were telling me something . . . and the intimidation. That was down to you.'

Sweet smirked.

Simnal stepped closer.

'Sir!' The nurse pushed his body between Simnal and Sweet.

'All right.' Simnal stepped back. 'But if I'm right, and I know I am, this means calculated premeditation. Just who have you got out there spying on me and my wife and son? I know how you work. Following me, then following my wife home.'

'Me . . . follow? Maurice, I have never left here.'

'You don't have to leave here, you and I both know that. You just say the word and it's done.'

179

'Sir! I insist.'

'Whatever it is . . . it's done. All right, I'm gone.' Simnal stepped further back. 'But just think what this means, Sweet. Just ponder the implications of long-term, planned, calculated premeditation. It was two, three weeks ago that you mentioned wanting a boy as a victim. It's in my notes. You have dug an enormous hole for yourself, an enormous hole, you with your need for accolade for your deeds.'

Sweet smiled, a 'you-can't-touch-me' smile.

'We'll see,' Simnal said. 'We'll see about that.' He pushed past Sweet and he and Roger walked to the door of the ward where the nurse tapped in the code at the controlled entry and allowed the door to unlock and Simnal to walk out into the warm evening air, though, once again, all he could feel was the cold.

The media, Simnal thought then and continued to think in later years, could not have been better. The press coverage of Toby's abduction was extensive, in the newspapers, television and radio. His smiling, freckly, face adorned posters in shop windows and public houses, in waiting rooms in bus and railway stations. The police too, he found, were excellent, particularly towards Jane, who blamed herself for allowing him to walk to the shops instead of accompanying him. A female police officer remained with her throughout. The only witness to the abduction was an elderly lady whose recollection was vague remembering a 'red car' and that 'the little lad seemed to know them inside', so she thought nothing further of it.

The next two days were days of self-reproach, fear, of imagining the worst possible outcome. He knew guilt in those days. All this came about because his marriage had failed because of his infidelity with a student. He told Tom Mautby of his conviction that Humphrey Sweet was behind the abductions, and Mautby and other officers interviewed him at length, but all they got from Sweet, Mautby reported to Simnal, was smirks and smiles and platitudes and denial. Above all, denial. Simnal could only wait at home, feeling impotent. Wanting the phone to ring, yet dreading what the news might be whenever it did ring.

It was the afternoon of the second day that Nora Worth glanced out of the window of her home and caught sight of a small head of blond hair, which appeared briefly at the upstairs window of the house opposite. She turned to the cage and said, 'Told you, Poppet, told you something was happening at that house.' She reached for the phone. Just thirty minutes later both he and Jane got the phone call that they had been praying for.

Simnal drove to Castleford Police Station where he was met by Jimmy Dancer.

'He was in Kathleen Hood's house,' Jimmy Dancer explained. 'The neighbour saw him. Who said nosey neighbours don't have their worth? There's just her and her budgie and she has nothing to do all day but watch the comings and goings in the street.' He opened a door for Simnal. 'Our sniffer dogs found something in her garden. We left a team digging there. It'll likely be the remains of Mr Hood. So a double result for us. Just down here.'

'Who abducted him?'

'Someone . . . someone you know.'

'Who? Why did they do it?'

'You can ask her yourself, if you like.'

'Her?'

'In the interview room.' Dancer stopped outside the door. 'Yes?'

'Yes,' Simnal said with determination.

Dancer tapped on the door and opened it. Simnal heard a male voice say, 'DS Dancer has entered the room. The time is seventeen fifty hours.'

Simnal followed DS Dancer into the room.

'The interview is suspended at seventeen fifty.' The

well-built officer switched off the tape recorder. Simnal saw the two police officers, a woman who was clearly a solicitor, and a fourth person.

'Why?' Simnal addressed the fourth person. 'Why?'

Ruth Day looked at him with pleading eyes and shook her head. 'Humphrey wanted it. We did what he told us to do, me and Kathleen . . . Humphrey wanted it.'

Simnal walked out of the room, feeling empty of stomach and weak of knee. He was reunited with his son in a softly decorated family room where he was playing with toys in the company of a female cadet. Toby ran to his father, who picked him up and said, 'Let's go and find Mummy, because we both love her very much.'

Epilogue

'So let us draw this to a conclusion.' The chairman spoke solemnly and looked round those present at the table. Simnal once again looked round the room, which was in the original, nineteenth-century, part of Kempton. It was the first time he had been in the room and was awed by its cavernous size, the abundance of richly polished oak panelling and the stained glass in the windows. He had been invited to the conference as a professional courtesy but because of his personal involvement, the invitation was conditional upon him observing, not participating. It was a condition Simnal had been delighted to accept. 'We are agreed therefore that Humphrey Sweet has not displayed any symptoms of a psychiatric illness whilst at Kempton. He may have convinced psychiatrists who interviewed him at the time of his arrest and prior to his trial that he was ill, but if he was, then symptoms would have emerged by now.' The chairman, tweed suit, bushy grey beard, paused. 'So we are agreed therefore that Mr Sweet is fully responsible for his actions and is therefore criminal?'

No one raised a dissenting voice.

'Good,' the chairman smiled, 'that will so be minuted and I will contact the Home Office by phone and then letter and request that Humphrey Sweet be transferred to the mainstream prison population.'

'When do we tell him, sir?' David Kehoe, the charge nurse, asked.

The chairman glanced at the senior police officer who was present.

'Not until the moment we are ready to move him, please.' He was a solemn-faced man and spoke with an equally solemn tone. 'That's the way of it in prisons, especially with dangerous prisoners, in case they try to frustrate their transfer. The Prison Service will need a day or two to find a suitable place . . . from here it will be either Durham or Gartree, I should think . . . but definitely maximum security.'

'Very well,' the chairman nodded. 'We'll wait until we hear from the Home Office or the police, but not to tell Mr Sweet anything until the police arrive at the ward to escort him.'

'Very good, sir,' David nodded. 'Understood.'

'We can afford to let him have a few more days in a soft bed.' The chairman leaned forward, forearms on the table. 'He'll be eating a lot of porridge before he breathes free air again. If ever.' He tapped the table with his pen. 'Meeting concluded.'